Blending heroic male icons, literary archetypes, gay relationships, and an observant, sharp humor, Jameson Currier's *Why Didn't Someone Warn You About Prince Charming?* collects twelve new tales of bad romances, backstage affairs, bittersweet recipes, and broken hearts.

"This collection is very much a tribute piece to the older gay man, the guy who has not achieved all of his dreams, but his power is in the fact that he hasn't given up—he's not down for the count, not yet. Where there's life, where there's love—there's still hope. There's still a life affirming story to tell."
—John Francis Leonard, *Lambda Literary*

"A smart, heartfelt set of tales of gay men's lives."
—*Kirkus Reviews*

"A writer who consistently surprises and delights, Currier's dynamism will surely carry his literary career to higher heights."
—*Bay Area Reporter*

Why didn't *someone* WARN YOU about PRINCE CHARMING?

stories

Jameson Currier

Chelsea Station
Editions

Chelsea Station Editions

New York

Why Didn't Someone Warn You About Prince Charming?
by Jameson Currier

Cover and book design by Peachboy Distillery & Designs

Published by Chelsea Station Editions
New York, NY 10018
www.chelseastationeditions.com
info@chelseastationeditions.com

Print ISBN: 978-1-937627-36-2
Ebook ISBN: 978-1-937627-79-9
Library of Congress Control Number: 2019946942

Contents

Why didn't *someone* WARN YOU about PRINCE CHARMING?

Lancelot's Secret

Lancelot has a foul body odor which Jeff, a chorus member in the touring production of *Camelot*, attributes to the actor's excessive sweating and unwashed costume. The stench bothers everyone in the cast, but everyone in the cast stinks when the proscenium lights of this giant auditorium flood the stage with heat. I told Jeff that this is nothing compared to the temperatures last week inside the workshop where the scrims and flats were painted for this production: a tin barn that trapped the Georgia sun like an oven. I gave up a paying job in retail to work for free this summer as an intern at this theater company in Atlanta. My job this week is much easier than the one before. Tonight, I wait in the wings of the theater and hand out ice cubes and wet towels as the actors leave the stage. A union concession allows me to stand behind the actors onstage for some of the production numbers. As a bonus, the stage manager lets me deliver a message to King Arthur in the final act.

My girlfriend Katie told me she liked a few things about this musical when she saw it the evening before. The songs were better than the one I worked on two weeks ago, where it sounded to her like everyone was talking too fast. She thought Lancelot was good looking, but that the costumes were silly. She thinks that I am foolish to be doing an internship in the theater, especially after her mother offered to get me an air-conditioned desk job at the insurance company where she works as an accountant. "And they made you wear tights!"

Katie said about my onstage professional debut. "But I could see your hairy legs through them!" She laughed and I realized she was laughing at me, as if my desire to be part of the theater is as ridiculous as running away to join a circus. Katie thinks the time I spend at the workshop, the theater, and with the casts of the touring productions that arrive weekly into town is a waste of the time that I should be spending with her.

But the joke is on her. Katie is not my girlfriend. Yes, we date. We go to the movies. I come over to her house. We listen to the cast albums I bring over to her house and we have sex in her bedroom. But if I had to say that someone was my girlfriend I would say it was Melissa. Melissa makes me smile. She makes me laugh. She likes musical theater. She understood all of the lyrics in the Sondheim musical two weeks ago and this week she swooned appropriately when she heard Lancelot sing.

But Melissa doesn't consider me her boyfriend. We don't sleep together. And she doesn't care about my internship at the theater, as if she knows something about me that I don't, in the same way that Jeff knows it. Jeff is in his late twenties, about eight years older than me and Katie and Melissa. He lives in New York, where he takes all sorts of acting and dancing classes. He told me he is waiting for his big break. So far he's been in the chorus of touring productions of *Annie Get Your Gun*, *Oklahoma!*, and *Hello, Dolly!*, which is how he was cast in this production of *Camelot*. When I am not watching Jeff dance, trying to figure out how his feet move from step to step, I am watching Lancelot. Lancelot is over six feet tall. Broad shouldered and dark-haired. He looks like a movie star and, according to the eye rolls I receive from his fellow cast mates when I ask details about him or his part, he already thinks he is famous.

Jeff is also friendly with Fred, the white-haired designer from New York who last week made the interns—all seven of us—paint in the wilting heat of the tin barn while he sipped ice tea. Jeff and Fred know each other through various Broadway theater connections. Last week, during breaks to cool down, Fred asked me about my college courses, if I did any sports, and if I was planning to come to New York to study theater. It did not surprise me to learn that Fred was a gossip. In the two months that I have been interning I have learned more about characters and personalities than I realized were possible, thanks to all the gossip and rumors that have found their way to me. Jeff knew everything about me when he stepped off the tour bus—that I liked to cycle, that my major is English, and that I want to move to New York. On the first night of the week of performances of *Camelot*, however, I learned that gossip can often be brutal, blunt, and hurtful. Fred said that Jeff was "out of step." His dancing is off the beat and not up to snuff and he might lose his job in the production. Fred also said that Jeff is struggling to get over a recent fling with the handsome actor who plays Lancelot. He looks at me to see how I register this news, but I only reveal my most nondramatic poker face that I often practice in front of the mirror in my bedroom.

* * *

I was eight when I first saw a live theater production at the outdoor amphitheater not far from where the tin barn warehouse is located. The next day I raided my mother's stash of cast albums and began playing them on the portable stereo in my bedroom. I wanted to be a singer because music brought to surface emotions that I did not know how to otherwise express. I was a lousy singer, however, not because I was overdramatic, but because I had no pitch or rhythm. I also failed at learning to play the piano, the guitar, and the trumpet. When I was cast as Rolf in our high school production of *The Sound of Music*, there was more drama backstage than on. I didn't know how to waltz and the girl cast as Leisl had to give me lessons. Katie and Melissa thought it was great that I was

11

getting dancing lessons, but Leisl's boyfriend threatened to beat me up if I kissed her. Kissing her was part of the script, however. A few days later I threw the first punch but earned some respect by making my stage debut with a busted lip.

When I arrive backstage at the auditorium where *Camelot* is playing this week, the production assistant in charge of work schedules for the interns hands me some cash and sends me out on errands. In the summer heat I drive my hand-me-down Buick Skylark to buy throat spray, lemons, and several specific items of make-up, which causes me some embarrassment until I ask an elderly clerk for help. She helps me find the right shades and brands of foundations, blush, and mascara that the actress who plays Lady Guinevere and the other cast members have requested. At least no one tells me it is my job to wash the stench from Lancelot's costume, though I hope it might be on someone's list.

A thunderstorm arrives when I park and make my way to the backstage door of the theater. The Southern humidity hangs heavily in the offstage areas. For my next assignment, I deliver messages and mail left for the cast, brushing the sweat that rivers from my face with the sleeve of my T-shirt as I walk through the airless hallways backstage. I think the actor who plays King Arthur is miscast; he looks more goofy than aristocratic and my mail delivery interrupts his nap. As he shakes himself awake, I apologize and leave his mail on a corner table of his dressing room. Before I leave, however, he grabs my wrist and looks at me the same way he looks at me onstage. He asks me if I pray regularly. I was saved and reborn when I was sixteen, around the time of the busted lip, but I no longer go to church and have collected plenty of sins since then. Jeff has warned me that Arthur's Bible-thumping behavior has alienated him from the rest of the cast, more so than Lancelot's foul-smelling costume.

"I should probably pray more," I tell King Arthur and realize I am bowing, as if I am onstage. When I upright myself, Arthur hands me a pamphlet with a dismissive, "You should read this."

I exit and stuff the pamphlet into the pile of messages and mail I still have to deliver and search the nameplates on the doors that match the remaining messages. I can smell the odor drifting out into the hallway when I stop at Lancelot's dressing room. I want to sneak a peek at what he is doing, but his door is closed and the stench is overwhelming, so I slip his mail through the crack between the bottom of the door and the floor.

My last mail stop is the dressing room I share with the guys in the chorus and the two other male interns. It is rowdy with laughter and talking when I hand out the mail because someone has received a newspaper that has listings of auditions in New York. Pages are tossed and snapped and handed around the room as though it was a map to buried treasure. Franklin, one of the chorus boys, lets out a wail when he discovers that the tour schedule will not permit him to audition for a role he feels he is destined to play.

Ambitions and jealousy roll into town with every cast. Jeff sums up behavior by lumping people into one of two camps: Arthur or Lancelot. Loser or Lover. Arthur sees this touring production as a pinnacle in his career of guest-starring sitcom roles. Lancelot is treading water for a better offer and rumors backstage are that he is about to land a TV series. Jeff hopes Lancelot will quit the show before it finishes its tour in Dallas at the end of the summer, not just because he is a jilted lover—that is something I am not supposed to know. And not because he hopes that a new Lancelot might get a better smelling costume. Lancelot's quitting will set in motion a rolling change in the cast of this production, which would allow Jeff the opportunity to get the big break he desperately wants, to move up and become a featured player, performing the role of Mordred.

Before half hour, I sit onstage with Jeff and he shows me his routine of stretches. He's full of advice and demonstrations—how to shake out your arms, how to wobble your thighs, how to get all the muscles loose and limber before the show begins. I think he likes touching me and moving my arms and legs into directions that don't feel entirely natural. But Jeff also wails about Lancelot. He asks me if I saw Lancelot talking with another actor after last night's performance. I see the tears well up in his eyes. I don't like seeing Jeff unhappy, so I ask him about his life in New York. How big is his apartment, where does he live, how expensive is it, and is it in a safe neighborhood? These are answers I am desperate to know. He answers tiny, West Side, too much money, and some blocks are really rough, especially late at night walking home from the theater. As we make our way up the stairs to the dressing room I overhear a heated conversation in the hallway between Arthur and Lancelot about religion and misplaced priorities. Seated in front of the mirror in the dressing room I practice my blank expression, thinking I might be the cause of the argument. Earlier, by mistake, I slipped Arthur's prayer pamphlet beneath Lancelot's door.

* * *

Because my schedule centers around the theater, I have not had enough time to spend with Katie. She calls me at my parents' house one morning and asks if I want to have lunch with her before I leave for my assignments at the auditorium. I drive to her house and we eat the bready sandwiches she has prepared. Her mother is watching soap operas in the den; her younger sister and a friend wander in and out of the kitchen giggling.

After lunch, we go to Katie's bedroom. I put an album on the stereo that I bought last week—a quartet who sing jazzy cabaret songs—and ask her if she likes the sound. She thinks it is too loud and she turns the volume down. She says that there is something wrong with her car—the Mustang her father gave her for her sixteenth birthday and which is now four years old—and would I go with her to the dealership so that she won't get ripped off by the mechanics. I suggest she get her father to take her because I know a lot about bikes but little about cars. I hate biking the roads in Atlanta—it's too dangerous—so I latch my bike to the back end of my car so I can cycle in one of the state parks north of the city. I can't get Katie to do anything sporty at all with me; she has no desire to bike or even hike the level trails. The only things she wants to do are shop and eat and see a movie if she has heard from one of her friends that it's good. Once, when I mentioned to her that I wanted to go to Europe because there were large cities where there are more bicycles than cars, her response was "Europe? Why would you want to be in Europe?"

That afternoon Katie tries to pin me down about getting together this weekend, but I haven't had any time to cycle and don't want that to make her more pouty, so I remind her that there are afternoon performances on both Saturday and Sunday and it will be difficult. I offer to get her another set of complimentary tickets to take her mom, but she only shakes her head no and her pouting expression turns to a frown. She has seen the show and doesn't want to see it again, which in my estimation is that she is only so supportive of the things I want to do and which to me is never supportive enough. But I never chased Katie. We became friends in high school because we sat opposite each other in History and English. In our junior year, she asked me to the prom. The summer after graduation, she asked me into her bed. I thought our fling would be over when we both went to separate colleges that fall, but Katie continues to seek me out wherever I live: on campus or at my parents' house.

Later, after the album has finished playing and we have had sex, Katie tells me she heard I saw Melissa last week. She is trying one more time to make me feel guilty about not being with her more. Melissa and Katie were never good friends in high school. Katie thought Melissa was loud and garish and uncouth. Melissa never cared what Katie thought about her, which only made Katie more annoyed. Last week, Melissa and I went to see an outdoor production of *A Little Night Music*. I was exhausted from working in the overheated tin barn, but I wanted to see how the musical was staged. Someone Katie knows must have seen us together.

I remind Katie that I've known Melissa longer than I've known her. Our families are neighbors. We grew up together. I walk out the front door of my parents' house and it is inevitable that I run into Melissa walking out her front door. Melissa attends an all-girl college in South Carolina and I seldom see her as often as I would like. I don't tell Katie that I'm not sleeping with Melissa because it is none of her business. I've never made a commitment to either one of them and I am beginning to question many things about myself, particularly my new sins, which I want to question in the privacy of my mind before I make any open declaration and face the wrath of more than just Katie. In an effort to change the subject, I remind Katie that the following week I will be painting flats and scrims in the overheated tin barn for the upcoming production of *South Pacific* and I won't be expected to be at the theater in the evenings. I don't say that I will spend more time with her then, but I let her think this may happen.

"Your frat brothers are gonna make so much fun of you when school starts up again," she says. "All this theater stuff."

I rise out of bed and look for my jeans and slip them on, ready to leave to drive to the theater, holding my expression steady and calm.

"You don't have to go yet," she says, with alarm. "It's still early."

It is not early and I am running late, but instead I answer, "Jeff told me that he would teach me some of the dance steps."

I sense her frown without even looking back at her. I say goodbye and don't wait for her to dress and let me out the door.

* * *

That evening after the performance Jeff asks if I want to join him and two other guys at a club down the street and I offer to drive the four of us in my car. I know of the club from my frat brothers—it's a club for gay men and the best place to dance because the room is large and open, the sound system is huge, and there is an operator who synchs the overhead rotating lights with the music.

A few of my frat brothers have taken their girlfriends to this club, but most of the girls felt uncomfortable there. I've been to this club a few times before with Mike, my roommate in the frat house. I'm not sure how to describe Mike. We're not boyfriends or lovers, though during the school year we are inseparable. We share classes, meals, pool time, and bike trips. We like the same kinds of books and music. I met Mike before we both pledged the fraternity our sophomore year; we were both cast in the chorus of the university production of *Damn Yankees*. It's safe to say that Katie is also jealous of the time I spend with Mike, though she thinks it is a platonic friendship. I wish I felt about Katie the way I feel about Mike, full of constant desire and joy when I am around him, and I wish I didn't have to keep this feeling hidden from everyone. Mike thinks that Katie is necessary, part of the larger plan, part of the secret even our frat brothers do not know about us since we keep our room and beds messy and unmade so it doesn't look like we are sleeping together. I haven't even told Mike about the true depths of my feelings for him, in part, out of fear that he might reject me if I said I was in love with him and I would lose what I have with him. This summer Mike is biking through Europe with the college cycling team, something I could not afford to do. I try to temper my disappointment that I am not with him because I don't like competitive biking. It's something I prefer to do slowly and for adventure. But the truth of the matter is I miss being with Mike, which often makes being with Katie more miserable.

At the club I dance with the guys from the cast, though I feel self-conscious because I am not a good dancer. It also reveals the awkwardness I feel about how I see myself. This world of gay men fascinates me as much as the theater does, but I have yet to figure out if I fit in and how. I don't want to be an actor; I haven't the training or the confidence for it. I like helping with building the sets, but I don't get the desire I feel when I am a part of the stories being told onstage. And I don't like that this secret world of gay men also comes with layers of shame, felony, and immorality attached to it by others. I don't like feeling that I am subhuman, mentally ill, or diseased. But most of all, I don't like keeping anything a secret.

But the music and the motion do wonders for whatever fears and hesitations I have. There are songs I've never heard before, the thumping bass pierces my body. I feel like I've wandered into a real version of Camelot and my poker face is forced into smiles. Jeff takes advantage of my mood when we dance together, grinding his hips up against mine. He stretches his long neck toward me, his nuzzling and groping becomes a rhythmic pulse. We stop dancing when the song begins to transition and he takes my hand and leads me to a corner where we lean against a wall and kiss. I'm startled by both my apprehensiveness at this public display of affection as well as the freedom I feel here to do it. I try to be oblivious of others as he kisses me but I can't. It's just who I am—someone who wants to take in as much of the world as is possible without missing a beat of it. Just when I worry that I will see someone I know I see someone I do know. My high school biology teacher, Miss Romero, is dancing with a group of women. As the startled fact rises to my consciousness—that Miss Romero might be a lesbian—even though I haven't seen her in more than four years—I realize that she would make a similar deduction about me—that maybe I am the gay one in the room, not her. But as much as I want to look away I can't. And that is when I see Melissa. She is one of the women dancing with Miss Romero.

A few minutes later the inevitable happens. Melissa blows me a kiss as her group moves to a space near where Jeff and I are entwined, as if she has known all along I have been here, and I give her a smile in return. And that is all that happens. No admonitions, no disapprovals, no drama or hysterics of betrayal.

I'm drenched with sweat when the lights flicker for last call. Out in the night, the air feels good against my damp skin, and Jeff slides his hand around my waist. The other cast members left earlier, so I drive Jeff back to the hotel where the cast is staying. In the parking lot when I stop the car, he leans over and gives me a kiss, and asks me to come up to his room. In the stairwell he tells me he is sharing the room with Andrew, one of the other guys in the chorus, but if we are quiet we will have some privacy in the bathroom.

Andrew doesn't stir in his bed when Jeff unlocks the door, and I drop my clothes on the floor where Jeff directs me to and I follow him into the small bathroom. His body is no surprise to me, I've studied it for days, but his cock is thick and stiff and a pleasure to touch and hold. We shower together for a long time, till we have both have come. In the dark room, in the hotel bed, we continue to quietly embrace and grope each other, and when Jeff climaxes again with a loud whispery gasp, I wonder if this is meant to wake Andrew so rumors will be spread backstage and find their way back to Lancelot.

In the morning, Andrew is not in the room, and sex with Jeff is more physical and loud. Later, after we have showered and dressed, he asks me to join him for breakfast and we drive to a place I know of on Peachtree. As Jeff talks about the songs he thinks he might use for his next audition, I am distracted by my own thoughts. Have I betrayed Mike by sleeping with Jeff?

What if Mike is having sex with someone on the cycling team? What should I say to Melissa the next time I see her?

Since it is a matinee day, I have to be at the theater early for errands, but Jeff says he can spend the time in his dressing room reading. At the theater, I use the backstage phone to call my mom and let her know I stayed at the frat house last night so she will not be worried. She tells me Katie has called several times and that I should give her call. But when I hang up I go about my errands, hoping that my silence and distance will send their own signals to Katie.

* * *

Backstage the heat and humidity are oppressive. Fans are set up in the hallway and electrical cords snake around corners. A stagehand raises a complaint about fire and safety hazards. Lady Guinevere vomits in her dressing room. When I deliver a bucket of ice to King Arthur's dressing room, he waves me inside, opens the lid of the bucket, and plops ice cubes into a large tumbler on the counter in front of his dressing room mirror. I place the bucket on the side of the counter and turn to leave, but once again, before I have left his dressing room, King Arthur has clasped me by my wrist to stay.

"The Scottish play is a soap opera compared to this travesty," he says.

"The Scottish play?" I answer as he twists my wrist tighter.

"The Bard's finest," he answers. "Shakespeare's tragedy. You know it is a curse to speak its name inside the theater. But at least the damned thing is thrilling to perform. Not like this bore. Never, ever, make the mistakes of *Camelot!* Every production I have ever been in has been cursed by something. Awful costumes, bad accents, thudding dances. I was once in an outdoor production where the director thought they should use live horses. The horses arrived onstage and crapped. At least it woke the audience up."

20

He lets go of my hand to pick up his tumbler and rattle the ice cubes against the sides of the glass. I can smell the sweetness of the alcohol seeping through his skin. "The Guineveres are hardly ever ladies. Bitches every one of them. Always think they deserve top billing. You know I am onstage more than any other character. I *am* Camelot. But the Lancelots are worse. Nancy boys with dirty little secrets. All of them sneaking around causing trouble."

There is a moment when he stops talking and I can see him drift into a thought about someone, or something. I make a motion to leave the room, when he takes hold of my hand again. "You know all about our young Lancelot, don't you?"

"His body odor?"

"He's cursed, you know. He's trying to poison all of us."

I can feel my face losing its blank expression as my mouth and eyes widen. "If there's a curse, how do you break it?" I ask.

He turns and looks at me as if he is only now aware that I am with him in his dressing room. "How do you break a curse?" he asks. "I should talk to Merlin about this!"

* * *

After the matinee performance, I am rinsing the buckets that I use to hold the ice chips when the stage manager finds me and tells me I have a visitor at the backstage door. I am surprised to find Katie waiting for me outside in the bright sunlight and heat, squinting and arms folded as if she is annoyed. I'm worried that she has heard something about me, something about the night before, but she gives me a kiss when she sees me and says she thought I might want to take a break and go with her to the mall nearby.

The mall nearby is always clogged with traffic and the trip would make me late for the evening performance, which is probably part of Katie's plan to get me fired so I will have to work for the rest of the summer at the insurance company, but instead I tell her I have a list of errands I need to run for cast members and ask her if she wants to tag along.

"Tag along?" she answers, as if I had said something offensive.

She suggests we take her car, but I'm concerned about her version of time and I tell her we will use mine. At the pharmacy down the street, we roam the aisles looking for items on my list. Katie has little enthusiasm for shopping when it is not shopping for herself, but she does make an effort to help me locate a specific brand of bandages that have been requested by the actor who plays Merlin.

Back in the car we drive to a nearby dry cleaner that is on my list of errands, where I hand the lady behind the counter a ticket for a pickup order.

She gives me a head tilt and says, "You're not the fella who dropped it off, are you?"

I shake my head no, and she disappears into a back room and emerges with a duplicate of the smelly Lancelot costume, only this one is clean and pressed and sheathed by a clear plastic covering.

"Tell your friend I was able to mend all the cuts," she says to me.

"Cuts?" I ask.

"I don't think they were tears," the lady says. "Looked like someone had a good time with a pair of scissors. Or a knife."

This seems to intrigue Katie. She says, "You mean, like someone was trying to tear up Lancelot's costume on purpose?"

"Is that what this is?" the lady laughs. "Well, I guess so."

* * *

Katie wants to know more about Lancelot. Who could possibly rip up his costume? I tell her that Lady Guinevere threw up after the matinee, and now she thinks there might be an unwanted pregnancy. She goes on and on about a theory that the actor playing Lancelot is really a bigger adulterer than the part of Lancelot.

In the parking lot behind the auditorium, Katie is asking me if I will come by her house after the show, when I see a taxi arrive near the backstage door. Jeff and some other cast members get out of the cab. He must have gone with the others to a restaurant nearby. Jeff notices me as he canvases the parking lot and sees that I am carrying a garment on a hanger.

In a few seconds he has jogged to where we are standing beside Katie's car, asking if I need help carrying any of the items I have collected inside. He sees that I have Lancelot's repaired costume and makes a move to take it from me, but I turn my body to prevent him, and in the process I introduce him to Katie. She gives him a curious up and down look, as if she is being judgmental, which she is, but she politely mentions she enjoyed the show when she saw it earlier in the week. There is a small moment of chitchat about the tour that I fear may take a bad turn if what I think is true, if Jeff was the person who cut up Lancelot's costume with a knife, and what he might now say about me to Katie, who may or may not have heard about my adventures with Jeff the night before.

I interrupt them and lean in and give Katie a fast peck on the cheek and say that I have to get inside, walking away before she can pepper me with more questions or look to Jeff for answers about my behavior. Part of me hopes that Jeff does say something about me to Katie, because it would make some things easier, but he jogs quickly to my side. When we reach the stage door he holds it open for me and again tries to take the repaired costume from me.

When I move away from his grasp, he says, "She's pretty. I guess she doesn't know."

"No," I answer curtly. "She doesn't. And there's no need to tell her."

* * *

No one knows who hacked away at Lancelot's costume or at least that is the version I get when the stage manager says that it was brought to him like that when the cast arrived in Atlanta, and it wasn't his job to pry into others' affairs, only to try to get it repaired or replaced. Whoever did it, probably also had a hand in the foul-smelling odor of Lancelot's duplicate costume. The stench doesn't come from Lancelot's body odor, or at least that is what I am led to believe. Something was poured onto it and trying to remove it only made the smell more foul. And rumor has it that Lancelot also has a nasty rash in an area where rashes can be really nasty.

But the word affair lingers in my mind as I make my way down the airless hallway delivering the day's mail and messages. Jeff is not over Lancelot. Katie can't let go of me. I can't let go of Mike. I worry I have made too many mistakes and maybe I should ask King Arthur to say a few prayers on my behalf or see if he thinks it might be alright if I drink my way to a conclusion. But thankfully his door is closed, and all I have to do is slide his mail beneath the door.

When I reach the men's chorus dressing room, Jeff is standoffish and doesn't want to have a conversation or limber up together. I wonder if it is because the others do not know the details of the damaged costume or maybe they do and this is the secret that binds them together and keeps them from telling me any of its details. I know I could get the answer from Fred, but I won't see him again until Tuesday when I'm working again in the overheated tin barn.

The curtain is delayed while the stage manager helps King Arthur sober up. Onstage, he slurs his speeches, forgets his lyrics, and wanders on and off stage whenever he wants. Several actors are forced to ad lib, but the audience remains clueless, and at the end of the show there is a standing ovation.

After the evening performance, I help the ushers clean the discarded programs from the front of the house, hoping to avoid Jeff and the rest of the cast. I'm relieved that when

I make my way backstage almost everyone has bolted from the theater as fast as they could and Jeff is not around. After finishing my last errands, it begins to rain when I reach my car. Heavy drops pound the ceiling of my car. I have no desire to track down Jeff, no desire to see Katie, no desire to drive back to my parents' house, so instead I sit quietly listening to the pounding rain, until I'm ready to drive to the frat house.

It's only a short trip from the auditorium to campus, though it seems like I travel through different lives to reach it. In the room that I share with Mike, I lie in my bed and try to detect his scent. I've avoided this room for most of the summer, because I fear it will make me obsessive and depressed, and when I feel I am headed in that direction I get up off the bed and leave the room, walking into a storage space at the backside of the frat house.

My campus bicycle is stored here and I unlock it from the grill and wheel it to a small workspace. I clean the frame and tighten the wires until I am tired and sleepy, then I crash on the sofa in the common room, where another guy is watching an episode of *Mary Hartman, Mary Hartman*.

* * *

Backstage is hectic when I arrive at the auditorium on Sunday for the final performance. Lancelot has flown the coup; he has been cast in a TV pilot that begins filming in Los Angeles on Monday. But I can't help being suspicious that there might be other motives for his hasty departure. Another secret behind the secret since Lancelot never wanted to be in Camelot.

But the chain reaction has been set into motion. There are quick meetings and fast rehearsals by the replacements in the cast. I follow a seamstress from one dressing room to the next with tape and safety pins to help her adjust costumes. The new Lancelot, an actor who was formerly in the ensemble, is too tall for the repaired costume, so the seamstress must camouflage her new rips and tears. Jeff avoids eye contact with me when I find him dressed in Mordred's costume and his hands flutter nervously as he practices his lines. I realize since I made my presence scarce the night before, he has moved me from his Lover column to the Loser one.

But the show goes on. A few lines are flubbed, an entrance happens on the wrong side of the stage, and someone loses a shoe during the dance routine for "The Lusty Month of May." One thing I have learned in these few short weeks: there is nothing professional about the professional theater.

After the performance I help distribute notes written for the cast by the stage manager about their stage missteps as everyone is changing and packing up their dressing rooms. King Arthur offers me a basket of fruit that has remained untouched in his dressing room all week. Lady Guinevere gives me an autographed headshot as an offer of thanks for helping her out with errands. The foul-smelling Lancelot costume is wrapped in sheets of plastic to be cleaned at the next tour stop.

Outside in the parking lot, I check off the names of the cast members as they board the tour bus for their next destination: Birmingham. When Jeff arrives, I congratulate him on his performance at the matinee. He was surprisingly good as the evil antagonist. But there are no hugs or displays of emotion between us; he does not even suggest that I look him up if I am ever in New York.

When the bus leaves and I finish my last errands, I drive my car to the state park north of the city where the flat terrain of the Georgia piedmont becomes lush, rolling hills. I park and unlock my campus bike from the rack on the back of my car. For hours I cycle along the trails, sweat soaking my T-shirt, imagining Lancelot on his way to a new adventure because he is no longer Lancelot, no longer destined to repeat the same mistakes, performance after performance. And so I pedal and coast, pedal and coast, determined to find my own path out of Camelot.

Superman Will Save Me

Superman was standing at the elevator when I walked over to the wall and pushed the up button. I tried to ignore him in the same way I ignored celebrities whenever they showed up to the downtown law firm to consult a lawyer: casting my eyes down to the floor, one hand in my pants pocket, the other grasping a folder or an envelope, my face reddening with embarrassment at being so close to someone so godly. I was twenty-three years old, a college graduate who had escaped his small Southern hometown for the big skyscrapers of Manhattan, and I had been working as a proofreader for only four weeks and not really certain of anything in my life except that the man I was avoiding looking at—hell, even avoiding acknowledging—was the Most Beautiful Man in The City of Beautiful Men—or at least the closest one in my immediate view. Superman was short, swarthy, and built like a bull. Behind me, I could sense his rising impatience with the elevator and he shifted his weight from one superhero leg to another and then stepped in front of me and pushed the elevator button again (as if that would speed things up). I swooned and studied his dark hairy forearm in my field of vision and then he mumbled something to me which I didn't understand.

Of course I didn't ask him to repeat it—whatever it was he said. It was something uttered in the language of the supergods and then filtered into English, something like, "Gotem chek dis, dunt eye drink." I used the moment, however, to look up from the floor and smile at him, taking in his big arms and meaty shoulders and the nipples clearly pushing their way through the fabric of the bright blue T-shirt he wore. Superman's real name was Spero Tzoumas and he was the building's handyman: the guy who was called when a conference room was too cold or a shelf was broken or a recessed light bulb in the ceiling needed to be replaced. The *super* man. The man who could fix anything. While everyone at the law firm, including us underling legal drones, were dressed up in high corporate drag (shirts and ties and suits), Superman went as casual as he could get by with. He got to show off his thick arms and pneumatic chest and which, as far as I could tell, no one ever objected to. (In fact, I swear some secretaries seemed to dress up for *him*—there was something that was not so casual about him which everyone seemed to tap into immediately—a raw sexual energy that even our celebrity visitors would often notice, their eyes wandering away from a meeting with a boring senior partner and widening with a "Who's that?" sort of delight at the sight of Spero standing on the fourth step of a ladder, his T-shirt creeping out of his jeans and revealing a superbly flat hairy stomach and the sleeves pinching so tight against his shoulder muscles that you just wanted to stop everything and lick his armpits.)

I didn't name him Superman. That nickname was given to him by Rick Cooper, my cellmate in the proofreading department. Cooper was in his early thirties but already balding and he wore thick black frame eyeglasses. He was a cynical, weather-beaten sort of man (wrinkled cotton shirt, former school tie at half mast, stained chino pants) who tried to make you laugh at his bitterness and world-weary experience (though I was so green and naive about most things, he would often have to backtrack and explain his remarks, which usually created another layer of cynicism and required him to pause to sigh and roll his eyes before he would decode his comments for me). Cooper and I sat in a windowless room on the twentieth floor of the law firm's skyscraper with nine other proofreaders where we were paired up into teams in soundproof glass-walled cubicles. Cooper had tidbits of office gossip on everyone on staff at the law firm—hence the nicknames, and this knowledge became a sort of short hand between us for Personal Case Record or Most Important Fault We Know About The Person.

In our department of glass cubicles there were The Golden Boy and The Baby Machine (a proofreader intent on being promoted to a paralegal position and his cellmate, a young woman who was hoping to get hitched to an attorney); The Paper Pusher and The Mall Dog (a team of two women, the first writing a romance novel while pretending to review contracts, and the other, a buxomy woman from the 'burbs who spent her commute teasing her hair); The Index Widow and The Idiot Without A Bite (a woman whose husband had died many years ago and who had made it her priority to remember every document our department worked on, and our senile and soon-to-retire supervisor, who was always disappearing to fix her false teeth). The attorneys, too, were not immune to Cooper's monikers. Our regular visitors included The Legal Drunk (a stooped, bow tie-wearing attorney who reeked of alcohol throughout the day and who had been relegated by the senior attorneys to reviewing Wills and Estates), the Scribbler (a curt-talking jock whose handwriting could never be deciphered), The Unfortunate Big One (an overweight attorney who had lost a case before the Supreme Court), and The Star Player (a fast-talking female attorney on a fast track to becoming partner—she was sleeping with a senior partner). Cooper had nicknamed me The Actor because he felt I was just doing time at the firm before I headed somewhere else, like an actor cast in a role and auditioning for another one. In fact, I had moved to the city with the hope of becoming an actor, even though I had neither the craft nor the talent nor the background experience to achieve that goal—my only desire was to be in the theater. After my first few disheartening auditions, I found my way to the want ads and this humongous multi-floor Wall Street conglomeration. But the truth of the matter was I *was* a good actor: I was also acting at being the type of guy who appeared he was comfortable around a type of guy like Superman, when, in truth, the honest-to-goodness truth, I was highly agitated to be there; I had moved to New York to be out and openly gay only to find myself nervous to admitting it because I found it could be a hindrance to getting a job in the theater or even at a Wall Street legal firm—and now I was as frustrated as I had been in my Southern hometown, wanting to meet someone exactly like him: *Superman*, a guy who could yank me out of the closet and save me from my miserable self.

So here we were, me swooning in front of the elevator button and Superman shifting impatiently behind me. The worst part of it was knowing we were about to share the same elevator together and I momentarily considered taking the stairs up the five flights to reach the office I needed to go to in order to return a rush job on a deposition just to keep from fainting in Superman's presence. Superman must have sensed my anxiety and he said something else to me, something like, "Aye kudye zwash ah clumb aye yuph."

When I turned around to him to acknowledge his comment (not that I understood a syllable of it), Superman was smiling and holding the hammer which hung from his tool belt and pretending to smash the door the down. I grinned and said, "Please, go ahead. Don't pretend on my account."

Just then the elevator door opened and The Unfortunate Big One got off, looked suspiciously at the two of us smiling and laughing, and Superman and I stepped inside. There were about three hundred other passengers in the tiny elevator cab who had been waiting forever to go up another floor and we wedged ourselves in, face to face. Superman was exactly my height, though about twice my size because of his musculature, and as the elevator doors closed it felt as if he were encircling my body to compress himself inside the small space. In front of me, his breath was warm and minty and I grew conscious about my own—I had onions on my salad at lunch—but Superman didn't seem to notice or he used his superhero senses to ignore my bad breath. I'm sure his X-ray vision could tell I was hiding a rising erection in my crotch and as the elevator went up another floor and the doors opened, we were pressed closer against each other as more passengers got in and out. As we rode and shifted, floor to floor, Superman continued his conversation with me, his voice whispery and moist and husky and flogging my cheek and chin and neck; by now we were certainly co-conspirators, ready to rid the firm of all evildoing attorneys.

When I finally reached my floor and left Superman behind, I was fully erect and using my interoffice envelope to hide my tenting crotch. A few minutes later, back at my cubicle, I was still flustered from the elevator ride with Superman and out-of-breath from taking an unventilated stairwell back downstairs to my floor. Cooper looked suspiciously at me and asked where I had been for so long, as if he had expected me to confess murdering an attorney and admitting my crime. I only briefly explained the elevator dilemma and patted at the sweat that was now pouring out of my brow. Then the phone in our cubicle rang and Cooper was talking with his wife and I was trying to ignore overhearing his conversation. She seemed to be one source of his weariness, or bitterness, or his miserable uneasiness, because there would be a long stretch when he was silent and then he would breathe in a deep sigh and whisper into the phone, "Okay, okay, all right, *enough.*"

Through our glass wall I could see The Idiot Without A Bite growing suspicious of Cooper's distraction from our work— we still had a new case brief to complete by the end of the day, so I turned my back to her and motioned to Cooper that he should end his phone conversation as quickly as possible. A few seconds later he slammed the receiver down, though he did not offer any explanation or apology for his aggressive behavior, and he started reading the brief out loud—very loud, word for word—while I marked the mistakes on my copy with a blue pencil. As the reading grew dizzyingly more boring my mind wandered to stay awake, and soon I was enmeshed in waves of confusion about where I had taken my life so quickly: into a too-expensive apartment, into a dull job, and into another situation where I wasn't able to talk truthfully about my sexuality. Cooper, too, grew more miserable and broody as the day went by, and as we were watching the last few minutes tick toward freedom, he asked me if I wanted to get a drink before I headed home.

I wasn't too keen on the idea; I wanted, really, to champion up the kind of courage needed to go into the type of bar that an unhappily married man like Cooper would have no interest in going to, but I knew I would probably pull my usual cop-out routine on my way home instead, wandering into the local newsstand and browsing through the gay magazines on their shelves, reading about and imagining the kind of life I desired to live, knowing that since I knew no other soul in the city except for the co-workers I had left safely behind in another part of town, the likelihood of being seen doing this activity was very minimal. So, as the elevator dropped us off in the big, shiny and expensive-looking lobby, I followed Cooper into a smoky bar two blocks away and we sat and had a few drinks. We talked about the low office morale, the strict employee policies which no one in management seemed to have a printed copy of, and soon, Cooper seemed to have gotten rid of all of his office gripes, and he started telling me I should take an acting class, one of those bohemian Village role-playing workshops which were so notorious for uncovering undiscovered talent, because (as he explained it) I had that sort of get-ahead, actory look about me. I told him that I wasn't an actory type of guy in the first place and then he segued into complaining about his wife, telling me that she could take a few acting lessons on how to pretend she could be marginally happily married.

"The biggest mistake I ever made was to get married," Cooper said.

"It can't be that bad," I said, trying to keep him more optimistic than dispirited.

"No," he said. "It was just the wrong thing for me to do."

Cooper really wasn't a bad guy. As far as I knew, he wasn't cheating on his wife, but after six years he'd had enough of her (or so he said) and he wanted out. I always felt there was a layer of sensitivity to his bitterness; didn't he have to feel good one way about something before he changed his mind and felt badly about it later? In fact, I wished he was the sort of man I could confide my true dilemmas to; were he gay, he could have been a guy who imparted pearls of wisdom to me from his own experiences. Instead, he drank and said, "Never get married. Live with a girl, sure, but never, *ever*, marry her."

I chuckled and wondered if Cooper had any clue to my own identity crisis and sexual awkwardness, and when I said, "Nope, no plans to do *that*," I could tell he wasn't really listening to the subtleties behind my answer; he had retreated again into the horror of his own affairs. The booze began to kick into my system, too, and there was a moment where we both seemed to lock eyes, and connect, look inside the other and find the truth behind each of us. I liked being with Cooper; I found his day-old stubble and wrinkled cotton shirt pleasantly thrilling. I wanted him to know more about me, just as I wanted to know more about myself—and how I might be *with him*. We left maybe one or two drinks later, and parted in the subway station. As I swayed and waited on the platform for my train, my courage evaporated and soon I was back in my apartment counting my pennies, wondering if I would have enough money to pay next month's rent.

The next day Cooper called in sick and I was forced to review documents with The Index Widow because The Idiot

Without A Bite was consumed with administrative details and final preparations for her retirement party at the end of the week. I sat in the Widow's cubicle with a headachy hangover and listened to her read legal jargon in an annoyingly high-pitch monotone, and when lunch time came around I wanted nothing but to nap in my own cube, but The Mall Dog was insistent that I join her in the cafeteria because she was The Kind of Woman Who Doesn't Like to Eat Alone.

She would not take no for an answer, so I went with her to the cafeteria and realized, while I was waiting in line to order a sandwich, that I was famished and perhaps my headache was more from hunger than hangover because I couldn't remember when I last had a decent meal. The Mall Dog flirted with the Hunky Hot Food Chef and got a pile high plate of French fries for the price of a side dish, and we sat at a table where she could look out at the other tables in the dining room. The Mall Dog wasn't really interested in anything I had to say and the truth of the matter was that I had nothing to say to her, so she talked a bit here and there about this and that about the office and her home life and her eyes darted from one table to another looking for someone she could snare into a real conversation. She spotted Superman leaving the cash register and waved him over to our table, and soon I was horrified to see him sitting opposite me, his huge, beefy arms squeezing their way out of the sleeves of that day's white T-shirt.

My stomach tumbled and my face reddened and I forgot how to chew, afraid of calling attention to myself and annoying the god who was now sitting directly across from me. My headache returned, roaring at full blast, and my brain yelled, *Get out, Get out, Get out of here as quick as you can*, though my heart was purring its usual confrontation, *No, you don't, you fool, stay, he's here, you'll get to know him better, this is the only way it's going to happen.*

The Mall Dog started right into a touchy-feely approach with Superman, tapping her red-painted fingernail against his plate, then feeling up his bicep and resting her fingers against his hairy wrist. I could not understand a word he was saying to us—he was talking about exercising, that much I deduced from The Mall Dog's questions, but the "kerb uhn prahtoons," and "doo hers bufire terk" were phrases that were easily lost to me in the blinding glare of the ever-widening headache. The Mall Dog had completely shut me out of her field of vision, but Spero refused to ignore me and devote all of his attention to her. (Yes, yes, yes, another one of his admirable superhero qualities, wasn't it?—Don't ignore the underling, no matter how *under* he is at the moment.) In fact, Superman seemed to use his X-ray vision in the same way Cooper used his bitterness—a knowing wink at the growing absurdity of office situations. When his eyes locked in with mine I felt certain that he was telling me that he was only pacifying her because he wanted to be with me. Me, me, *me. Silly confused me.*

I had no concept of how to flirt with a man, particularly in a work situation or even if I should because it would surely get me fired and I was always desperate for money, living paycheck to paycheck, so I sat there and let The Mall Dog do all the work for the both of us, drinking in the details of Superman as he turned away from me and said something to The Mall Dog before returning and locking eyes again with me. While The Mall Dog fed Superman French fry by French fry from her plate, I studied his hands and fingers and palms and wrists (short and stubby but well-manicured) and wondered if what I had heard from my school days were true—that finger size was an indicator of cock size. Then I remembered that it was nose size and not fingers which were supposed to be the revealing factor, so I studied Spero's nose, thinking about how big and large it was and how well it must reflect his other body parts. His eyes were ringed with thick, curly back lashes—top and bottom—that The Mall Dog must certainly be coveting as well, and his eyebrows stretched into one another above the bridge of his nose. I thought some more about his nose and then thought about his shoe size—another myth I had remembered hearing of, and I nodded to him when he turned and said to me, "Duht ahm eyeuh zuposhed do doah? Suhs zuk eye dees duh meee."

Again, I nodded, now thankful my lunch break was finally over and my heart beat could resume its normal pace, and I spent the rest of the day asking around for pain relievers and trying to avoid The Mall Dog's neediness to recap and deconstruct the lunch to gauge Superman's interest in her. (She, too, was single and husband hunting; hence the highly teased bouffant she felt could attract those men without the benefit of super-vision.) Cooper was back in the office the following day, as bitter as ever, and the rest of the week flew by with one case brief after another and ended with a celebrity sighting when a tennis star showed up to initiate a new foundation for weary muscle joint victims, which all of us office drones were worried would delay our impending departure to The Idiot Without A Bite's retirement party.

The retirement party was a big affair at a nearby downtown club the firm had rented for the evening: they had gone all out with a DJ, an open bar, and hors d'oeuvres of shrimp, salmon, scallops, and other unidentified mysterious seafood. It wasn't a mandatory affair but since The Idiot had been with the firm for more than three centuries, as far back as when the founding attorneys had arrived on the Mayflower, it was obvious that it would be a well-attended affair, with most of the senior management and partners of the company present (and any and all absences certain to be noted in future performance reviews). But it was also an excuse for everyone to overindulge in the company of everyone else, as well as doing so and escaping the detection of day-after hangovers in the office. There was wide selection of quality booze for whatever cocktail you wanted to construct and the club had a big sound system and a tiny dance floor, to encourage misbehavior and fuel more office gossip that could (hopefully) be forgotten by the end of the weekend.

I walked over to the party with the rest of my department and sat and had my first drink (a White Russian) with Cooper, who nursed a Gin and Tonic and complained that his wife was pestering him about investing in a house and which would mean a longer commute for him. Cooper was miserable talking about his wife and I sensed that they would probably never make it to a new house *together*. The Mall Dog joined us for our second round and did her best to try to convince one of us to dance with her ("I'm not a Woman Who Enjoys Dancing Alone..."), but she was unable to persuade either of us to shed our inhibitions, which was when Superman made his entrance at the club, wearing a tight black T-shirt and black jeans, and The Mall Dog departed to snare a more willing victim.

I tried to ignore the fact that Superman was present and the sexiest thing I had ever seen and could not see enough of, but after a while I left Cooper with The Scribbler, who had wandered over to us to relay a surprisingly long-winded anecdote about a client, and pretended to nosh on chips and peanuts while watching The Mall Dog outrageously flirt with Spero. I knew I was out of my league lusting after him, out of my league thinking that I could find happiness at this job and in this sort of place. Cooper was right in a way, I was only playing a part, my days at the firm were numbered, though I still hadn't a clue of anywhere where I wanted to go, only that I wanted to be somewhere other than here. When The Baby Machine showed up at my side and said that I shouldn't be drinking alone at a party, I joined her and The Golden Boy for another round, though found myself alone again when the two of them headed for the dance floor.

That was about the time all the booze kicked in and I felt a bit wobbly and made my way through the dark club to find a toilet. Things weren't really spinning, spinning, spinning, but I was experiencing one of those inner body moments when you think your life is as wonderful and scary as a roller-coaster ride in a defunct amusement park.

I was standing at the sink splashing water on my face when Superman flew into the restroom. He looked at me looking at him in the mirror and threw his beefy arms out from his body and said, "Aye, vuht lark doah zeuh ooye harh." He clearly had had more to drink than I had and he wobbled to the urinal—it was a tiny restroom—one urinal, one sink, one stall (which was occupied)—and unbuttoned his jeans and pulled out his cock. I tried not to look, really I did, but I truly, certainly, and desperately, wanted to know all I could about The Thing I Had Fantasized About For So Long, and, in my over-inebriated state, I must have widened my eyes when I caught sight of his true gift—a magnificent Super-Tool worthy of a superhero. Superman shook out the last drops with a flick of his wrist, but he didn't put his Super-Tool so quickly back into his pants. Instead, he started stroking it and we both watched it grow larger and larger and his moaning become louder and louder.

At some point my breath stopped—I was certain I was about to faint from ecstasy—but instead I watched him use his free hand to brace his weight against the tile wall. He bowed his head toward his Super-Tool and muttered something like, "Gotem jheck dis gerged duyup."

He started breathing through his mouth and letting out deeper pitched moans and I completely forgot that we were not alone in the room—the stall was still occupied by someone who was now on their knees, his head over the rim of the toilet and emitting tiny gags and barfs as if he were sick and throwing up. Superman heaved his chest up and down and clattered his fist against the tiles and the back of his neck reddened and then he tensed his body and shot into the urinal. His breathing slowed down, he shook the last drops out into the porcelain bowl, and behind me the Unknown Man gagged again and flushed the toilet. Superman crammed his God-given gift back into his jeans and buttoned himself up. I moved away from the sink as he stepped forward and ran his hairy hands beneath the water and scrubbed them the way a doctor would clean his hands after surgery, unwinding a long set of paper towels and drying himself off, then checking out his face in the mirror. Before he left the room, he looked at me and grinned, his arms going out wide out to his side and he said, "Duhm lark dush gey seehad." Then he took both palms and pressed them against the sides of my neck, as if he were going to crush my skull. Instead, he drew me into the deepest, most luscious kiss I had ever known. Here, in the beefy embrace of a superhero with his tongue searching out my tonsils, I was finally certain my life was beginning.

Behind us, The Unknown Man barfed again and flushed the toilet and then I blinked my eyes and Superman was gone from the room, as if kryptonite had been discovered and he had flown away to safer ground. I walked outside the bright room, into the dark and noisy air of the party. I know my steps must have faltered a bit, dizzy from the kiss, my eyes adjusting to the dim colored lights of the club, the booze still swirling through my veins. Through the foggy blur in front of me, I saw Cooper approaching in my direction, probably to ask me if I wanted another drink. The next thing I knew he was standing right in front of me and whispering in my ear to ask if I wanted to dance.

I leaned back from him, ready to say, "With you? What would everyone say?" but he wouldn't let me get the words out fast enough. In fact, his mouth was there, right in front of mine, and in front of everyone still at the party, drunk and ignoring us anyway, he kissed me and tucked his hands around my waist. I tried to pull away from him to tell him something, God knows what, that I was ashamed that I had the hots for Superman knowing full well he wasn't about to make me his Lois Lane, and that I had no clue that he—Cooper—could possibly have felt this way about me because he never gave me any sort of Important Clue, but instead all my words and thoughts became garbled inside Cooper's mouth, and they sounded guttural and primal, like I was saying, "Gotem eyah fuldah bahek."

I stood there thinking that there would be some awkward moment of realization between the two of us—Cooper and me—but there wasn't one because it felt so natural to be in his arms. Cooper was suddenly tall and strong and capable of leading the way I wanted to go at that moment. In fact, he let me kiss him again while we stood swaying back and forth, pretending we were already on the dance floor.

"Maybe we should get another drink somewhere and talk about stuff," he said. He pressed his forehead against mine. His breath was hot and moist.

"Okay," I answered. "I'm steady now."

And then he took my arm as if he thought I was just pretending to be drunk and he draped it around his shoulder, as if he were drunk too, and we stumbled and swayed together as if we were both pretending each other was too drunk to stand without the other. Together we stumbled out of the club and into the thick air of the night, giddy and happy, the two of us imagining we were finally free, flying through air, our Big New Adventure already begun.

Sometimes You Have to Settle for Popeye (Even Though You'd Rather Play with Bluto)

You hate the beach. You hate the sun and the squinting and the sweating and the sand sticking to everything. Everything is too hot and bright. Your friend Jesse loves the beach. Jesse sits in his beach chair under the shade of his umbrella that you have carried for him from the parking lot, across the hot sand, and shoved into place. Today there is no breeze. The flies are the size of golf balls. You look out at the horizon and want to fall asleep. You pretend you are comfortable on your towel, though Ella, Jesse's dog, takes up most of the shade. You are Jesse's guest for the weekend. Jesse's free labor and dog walker. You have driven Jesse, his dog, and his suitcase three hours from the city in a rental car through heavy traffic. This morning after you walked the dog and washed up from cooking breakfast for Jesse and two of his housemates, you packed lotion, water, books, magazines, and a pooper-scooper for the beach.

Jesse has chosen a spot on the beach near a gay couple he has met before. "They know everyone," he said when he spotted them from the top of the dunes. Jesse is husband hunting. He wants to meet a wealthy professional which is why he has chosen to take a share in a weekend house in the Hamptons and not Fire Island. Jesse is a romantic, not a realist. He wants

41

a man who will take care of him, take him to the theater and on exotic vacations, and buy him a weekend house, not a guy who will wander off to the dunes the moment he unfolds a beach chair.

The couple he sits next to are a doctor and a lawyer. They both went to Ivy league schools. They are both tall, have long, wavy hair, and bright white teeth. They are both the type of guy Jesse wants to meet and marry. "Only if they were twenty years younger," Jesse whispered before he sat in his beach chair and forgot to introduce you to them.

The couple makes small talk with Jesse before they ignore him and settle back into their books. Jesse pretends to do a crossword puzzle. You flip through the pages of a magazine, swiping away at sand. Ella pants heavily. You think she hates the beach as much as you do.

Jesse wants to know who everyone is on the beach and what their backstory is. The couple beside him refuse to gossip. They respond with unopinionated answers. "He lives in the Springs." "He works in Amagansett." "I believe he's only out from the city once a month."

Jesse is clearly bored and frustrated but aware that he must show some manners to the couple if he wants to dig deeper into their address book of potential husbands. He is grateful when he sees his housemate Brad walking along the surf. He waves Brad over to his chair. This is Brad's fourth year doing a summer share in the Hamptons. He knows the gossip and is willing to dispense all of it. Jesse pumps him for info as Brad sits on your towel and scratches the dog's head, pushing you a little further out into the hot, cancerous sunlight. Your eyes flutter with exhaustion from doing nothing. When a gorgeous dark-haired man with the physique of a bodybuilder jogs by wearing only a skimpy swimsuit, Jesse must know everything about this god.

Brad says he is a local carpenter who goes both ways. "AC/DC." Then adds, "Popeye knows him."

"Popeye?" the couple beside us echo.

Jesse is annoyed the couple was ignoring him but obviously eavesdropping on his conversation with Brad and responds with a flurry of waving hands that playfully slap Brad's arm. "It's an inside joke," Jesse says to the couple. Now it is his turn to be tight-lipped.

Brad rises and says to Jesse, "We're all sitting down there." He points to a tiny cluster of umbrellas in the distance. "Why don't you join us?"

Not willing to impolitely abandon the couple that ignores him, Jesse says, "We're leaving soon. It's too hot for Ella."

You look at your watch and see you have been at the beach less than a half hour. Suddenly, you are grateful for the snobbish older couple.

"See you at the pool," Jesse says before Brad is out of earshot. He turns to the couple and says as he clutches his beach bag, "You must visit our house and see the pool. It has a waterfall instead of a diving board."

The couple give Jesse weak smiles and say, "We know the place." They return to their books. The dog is already running back to the parking lot before you have finished shaking the sand out of the towel.

* * *

"He's not for you," Popeye says to Jesse. They are sitting on the deck by the pool and talking about the AC/DC carpenter.

Jesse is infatuated with the carpenter. He wants to know more about him. There is a rumor that he was working on one of the houses south of the highway on the pond and sleeping with both the owner and his wife. Popeye veers the conversation back to Jesse, which is an easy feat. Popeye has a crush on Jesse. Popeye is not his real name. His real name is Gary but Jesse refers to him as Popeye when Gary is out of earshot or out of sight. Jesse gave him the nickname because

Gary is short, pale skinned, and has big forearms and a quick, high-toned laugh that sounds like a cartoon character.

"How do you know what I want?" Jesse says, laughing.

"It's written all over you," Popeye says. Gary is a music teacher. He lives in New Jersey and has a full share in the house. He is off for the summer and out east all the time. You think Jesse underestimates Popeye. Popeye has a handsome face and a cheerful personality. He's a do-er not a show-er, unlike Jesse who wants to be waited on and adored all the time. Jesse loves show tunes and wants to be a cabaret singer though he cannot hold a pitch, so instead, Jesse writes reviews of plays and musicals and interviews cabaret stars. He thinks what he really wants to be is a director or producer, even though he has no experience, only a lot of family money he can spend. You think Popeye is perfect husband material for Jesse. They could sing show tunes all the time. Jesse wants a professional husband he can show off on opening nights. He's made it clear that he could never survive on a teacher's salary.

Gary swims in the pool. He has a nice, toned body, not over-pumped from a gym membership. Jesse is chunky and hairy and won't take off his shirt. He expects to find a boyfriend on the sheer force of his personality. You'd love to be with a dreamboat or porn star, though you'd rather spend time with a best friend who comes with perks.

Food arrives when the rest of the housemates have returned from the beach and shopping. Chips are in bowls. The barbecue is turned on. Popeye pours cocktails and brings them poolside. Jesse sips and wants to know if the housemates have any rich, single friends.

"When's dinner?" he asks, when you put the leash on Ella to take her for a walk.

* * *

You are the designated driver. You drive Jesse, Brad, and two other housemates to the dance club on the highway. Jesse positions himself near the door so he can see who arrives and leaves. Jesse doesn't want to dance because he doesn't want to get sweaty. If he gets sweaty, he will be cranky. If he is cranky, no one will fall in love with him from the sheer force of his personality.

You dance with Brad and another housemate. Popeye arrives and talks to Jesse. When Jesse refuses to dance, you dance with Popeye. When the song finishes you go together to the outdoor seating area. The AC/DC carpenter sees Gary and gives him a hug. Standing together, they look like live-action versions of Popeye and Bluto. Gary introduces you to Paul, the real name of the live-action version of Bluto. In high school, you used to work in a hardware section of a department store, so you know a few things to keep a conversation going with a carpenter. Paul is talking about the poor quality of the paint on the outside deck of the club when Jesse arrives. He tries to flirt with Bluto but Bluto does not want to talk about show tunes.

Instead, Paul asks you to dance. As you head to the dance floor, the shock on Jesse's face is burned into your consciousness. When the song ends you walk together to the outside deck. Jesse and Popeye are nowhere to be seen. You see a couple of guys head out into the row of bushes behind the deck where it is dark. Bluto says it's a big cruising spot. "Hold onto your wallet," he says and takes your hand and leads you into the darkness.

* * *

When you return to the club the dance floor is packed. A popular disco song is playing. The disco ball is spinning. Men are dancing shirtless. Everyone is sweating. Except Jesse. Jesse spots you immediately and whines in an octave decibels above the dance music, "Where have you been?" You point from the direction you came from, but he doesn't care about your answer. He is ready to leave.

Your ears are ringing and your clothes smell of cigarette smoke. Jesse is unhappy that he did not meet anyone up to his standards. He is annoyed that Bluto gave him the cold shoulder. "A carpenter," he says in a tone of someone who has had too much in life too soon. You don't tell him about your adventures in the bushes.

Back at the house Jesse has another drink while you walk the dog. He is passed out when you have finished with a shower and are dressed in a clean T-shirt and shorts. You fall easily asleep. You don't even hear the housemates arrive and shower and flush.

* * *

Early the next morning, you take the dog for a walk through the neighborhood. It is full of houses you think you will never be able to afford. Lawns are beautifully manicured. Flowers and shrubs are thick and green and in bloom.

Back at the house, Brad and Popeye are in the kitchen.

"So you discovered the bushes!" Brad says and hands you a cup of coffee. You roll your eyes to the bedroom upstairs and say, "I don't think Jesse knows."

You sit and talk for a while about the club and gay life in the Hamptons, then read the Sunday newspaper. After a while you walk upstairs and check on Jesse. He rolls over in his bed, looks at you, and says, "I don't feel so good. We'll drive back tomorrow. Is that okay?"

You nod but before you leave the room, Jesse says, "Why don't you spend the day with Gary? He thinks you're cute."

You smile, feeling as if bought a winning lottery ticket.

You find Popeye out by the pool and ask him if the bikes in the basement are in shape. He says the tires need air, but there is a hand pump in the house. You ask him if he wants to bike into town. He slips on a T-shirt and shorts and helps you find the pump.

The bike ride is glorious. The air is thin and crisp. Popeye tells you about the way sunlight hits this part of the island, why the area is full of so many painters and artists with homes.

The town is busy but not crazy. You buy Ella an expensive designer dog biscuit from the pet store. Popeye buys a pair of flip flops he can wear out by the pool. Together, you sit outside the deli and watch expensive cars drive by. You are impressed that Popeye knows makes and models. He talks about growing up in California before his family moved east because his father got a teaching job at a college in New Jersey.

Back at the house, housemates are packing and checking the train schedules. Jesse is still in bed. You ask if he needs something to drink or to eat or any medicine. He answers, "A migraine. I just have to let it go away."

By late afternoon the house is empty except for you, Jesse, Popeye, and the dog.

You heat a pizza in the oven and watch a movie with Popeye. He joins you for the dog's evening walk. While you are outside in the darkness, he takes your hand and draws you into a kiss. "I've wanted to do that since yesterday," he says.

Upstairs, Jesse is snoring. You settle into Popeye's bed. It's narrow but plenty of room for what you both want.

You love summer. You love the Hamptons. You love being loved.

Sometime in the middle of the night the dog finds you with Popeye. He leaps up onto the narrow bed and settles between your legs. Popeye stirs and draws you in closer. He understands this is where the dog would rather be.

Mr. Darcy's Pride

The problem begins with Mr. Darcy, as all problems do, though it was Mr. Bingley who surfaced the predicament.

"If it's true, you're fired," Nancy Lee says.

Nancy Lee is my boss. We are seated in the back room of the office suite where we work and where private conversations are held, away from the continually ringing phones at our desks. Her business partner, Nina, also her "partner" in her private life, is seated beside her, glaring at me with squinty, suspicious eyes. They are Sutton Place butch and femme, swaddled in silk and jewels, an older generation of swanky uptown women in their fifties next to my scruffy, young downtown hedonist. I am dressed in jeans and a shirt I purchased when I was still in college, four years before, when I could afford to go shopping because I thought student loans were gifts. We are the entire staff of a public relations firm handling four Broadway productions, three celebrities, and two nightclubs. I do everything in the office the elder Park Avenue lesbians don't want to do, which is pretty much everything except gossiping and talking on the phone with celebrity newspaper columnists. I type press releases on stencils, ink the mimeograph machine, print the releases, fold them into envelopes I have addressed, and carry them to the post office to mail. Every morning when I arrive I make coffee, look through six newspapers and seventeen magazines for clippings, tearing out articles and reviews to photocopy and send to clients. I should probably add it is a rainy March morning when I am summoned into the back room for this private conversation; I am still damp from walking thirty blocks from the West Village to Times Square because using my hard-earned pennies for a subway fare seems like a luxury to me.

Seated opposite my accusers, several thoughts go through my mind. If I am fired I will likely abandon the completion of a union apprenticeship, two of three required years tossed down the drain trying to gain professional experience to become a card-carrying bona-fide theatrical publicist. If I am fired I will also not be able to pay the rent on my tiny Greenwich Village apartment, not exorbitant by Manhattan standards, but high-priced because I am straddled with the student loans which I also used to finance my move to New York and my sub-professional pay. But if I were to lose this job it could also be a way to extricate myself from what I feel is a lousy profession and an even lousier job. I never wanted to be a publicist. I hate being in the middle of everything and everyone: demands and counter-demands between clients and the press, producers and actors, critics and audiences, Sutton Place lesbian against Sutton Place lesbian. And I hate faking being interested in things I think are crummy and sub-par; in the three years I have worked in this office we have been hired to flog one turkey after the next, including an off-off Broadway debut of a former Scandinavian beauty queen who doesn't speak English in a play written by her lover, who doesn't write in the sort of English an audience can understand. It is never a surprise to me to hear that our office has as bad a reputation as the one Nancy Lee has just accused me of: sleeping around to get ahead. On this rainy March morning, in the back office, Nancy Lee explains that she has heard that I am having an affair with an actor in a show we represent: Mr. Bingley to be precise, in an awful, three-hour musical adaptation of the Jane Austen novel, *Pride and Prejudice*.

As I look from butch to femme several thoughts go through my mind: My bosses are sleeping together so why are they so hostile about my own sex life? A producer and the stage manager are sleeping together. Nancy Lee's former lover, a newspaper gossip columnist, is also having an affair with an actress in the show. Another actress is doing escort work on the side. It seems like a double standard is being applied to me: a twenty-six-year-old gay male apprentice in a theatrical publicity office, now becoming a victim of malicious theater gossip.

One thing I have learned from being an apprentice, however, the less you say, the better off you will be. But I don't often remember it. I also happen to know some gossip about Nancy Lee. Barry, the co-producer of the soon-to-be mega Jane Austen disaster, is threatening to fire her from the show.

"My personal life is personal," I say to my accusers. "It's none of your business."

"It is when it affects our business," the unpleasant femme partner hastily answers.

"Is it true?" Nancy Lee asks again.

"If you want the answer, you will also have to bear the consequences."

I realize I sound too much like a Jane Austen character, but my tight diction serves the purpose.

"You're threatening us?" the femme partner asks, the volume of her voice higher and louder and more accusative than it usually is.

"There are plenty of scandals I think the press will love to hear."

"He is threatening us!"

"I could stop you," Nancy Lee says. "Have the pieces pulled."

"Only the ones you know about."

"Is that a threat?"

"No, it's business," I answer. "Nothing personal."

* * *

I am not fired because I do not admit to anything and am needed because the opening of *Pride and Prejudice* is one week away, hardly time for the two women to find and train a replacement for me. I spend the day at my desk shaky and angry, the phone ringing constantly about requests for tickets. After I finish office hours, I deliver the house seat orders, press lists, and interview requests and memos at theater box offices and back stage. At the theater where *Pride and Prejudice* is in previews, Steve is in the backstage stage manager's office on the second floor.

"Nancy Lee wants to fire me," I tell him.

"That makes it easier than quitting," Steve says. "And you can get unemployment."

Steve is a half-foot taller than I am, which makes him slightly over six feet. He's lean and thinly muscled like a basketball player, and has the kind of shaggy curly mop of hair I wish I had. My hair is more frizzy than curly, especially on rainy days like this one. Steve has also got four years on me, so he is already deemed to be an experienced theatrical professional, having been an assistant stage manager on a few workshops and off-Broadways gigs. I first met Steve at a men's bathhouse in Chelsea and he lived with me for a few months when he was between shows, which meant that we had sex several times. He recommended me to a trick who recommended me for a job opening at Nancy Lee's office, which is how I became a wannabe press agent, though Nancy Lee and her partner are not aware of that sexual backstory.

"There's a lot of gossip going around," I tell Steve. "She thinks I am sleeping with someone in the show."

"Are you?" Steve asks. There is a slight tone of worry in his voice, as if I am stepping into territory that I don't belong in, *his* territory.

Pride and Prejudice is Steve's first Broadway show and his first time in charge as the stage manager. Barry, the co-producer, is also Steve's boyfriend, which means that they are living together and should be having a lot of sex with each other. Steve, however, is having an affair, or, rather, continual sexual relations, with the actor who plays Mr. Bingley. Mr. Bingley, in fact, is causing quite a stir.

Mr. Bingley describes himself as a nudist, though I think narcissist would be a better description. He is originally from California where you can easily get away with both of those monikers. Even if he wasn't from California he could get away with it because of his looks. Mr. Bingley is closer to Steve's age than mine and is also over six feet and nicely muscled, in a rugged, leading man way. Mr. Bingley wanders around his dressing room in the buff which means he has assumed the scrutiny of many in the cast and their visitors. Mr. Bingley is also extremely well-endowed, often to the point where his handsome face, hairy chest, plump biceps, and furry thighs go unremarked. Because he refuses to wear any undergarments beneath his period costume when he is onstage, Mr. Bingley's appendage has assumed a starring role in the production, much to the delight and dismay of many.

Discussions have been had between the director, costume designer, dresser, and Steve, all in an effort to mask Mr. Bingley's pronounced endowment while he is performing on stage, all to no avail. When Mr. Bingley arrives onstage, so does his unharnessed appendage. It flops and flaps for three hours, often causing distractions both of the audience and the cast and certainly to the well-heeled plot of the masterpiece. It has also distracted Steve from Barry. Privately, Steve told me last week during the first days of preview performances that he thought that if he provided Mr. Bingley with a little personal attention prior to going onstage, perhaps his appendage would recede into the background of the costume. No such luck. As Mr. Bingley enters and exits his scenes he passes by Steve at his stage manager podium in the wings and his desire swells further.

"I'm not the one gossiping," I answer Steve, though his response is to look away from me and pretend to do stage manager tasks.

All of this, of course, is doing damage to Mr. Darcy's reputation. Mr. Darcy is also from California, having made a name as the action hero star of a high-grossing Hollywood movie. Mr. Darcy, in fact, is also well endowed, yet he is not as handsome or tall or young as Mr. Bingley and this has caused some friction. In his Hollywood hit, Mr. Darcy has no hairline and a beautifully shaped and polished forehead and skull that shines with sweat. In *Pride and Prejudice*, Mr. Darcy wears a hairpiece that looks like a hairpiece and which has become as much of an item of discussion as Mr. Bingley's endowment. No production photos have been approved because of Mr. Darcy's vanity. During previews last week several different hairpieces made cameo appearances, all to failed acclaim. This has caused Mr. Darcy to become jealous of Mr. Bingley and the attentions he has been receiving because of his appendage. In an effort to remain noticed in the production, Mr. Darcy has also taken to flapping and flopping his endowment for three hours on stage, to such great arcs and swings that it sometimes seem that the appendages are now doing the finer bits of acting.

Mr. Darcy's jealousy has also extended to off-stage matters. He has essentially decided he is a) in the wrong project, b) in a lousy show, and c) looking for a reason to get out of it. Many in the cast and crew think he is personally sabotaging the show. Just like he refuses to be photographed, he refuses to do any interviews, much to the distress of members of the press eager to know what it is like for a big Hollywood action hero to be trapped in period costumes and a toupee. Mr. Darcy, however, is fearful that all of the sexuality and bravado on stage will reveal all of the sexuality and bravado off-stage. For years, Mr. Darcy has dodged rumors that he is gay and that he lives a closeted life with an equally closeted wife and lovers. He has even threatened to sue one notorious tabloid to prove his point.

* * *

Backstage, Steve defends his position, or, rather, his services. It is keeping Mr. Bingley and the audience happy. He overlooks mentioning his own satisfaction and I avoid mentioning that Nancy Lee thinks I am the one having sex with Mr. Bingley. I look at my watch and think I have time to talk to Mr. Bingley. I find him in his dressing room, standing nude before the rack with his costume. He smiles when he sees me and I notice his appendage stir.

I apologize for the intrusion and then launch into matters. "There's some confusion," I tell Mr. Bingley. "I shouldn't be here. But I thought you might help clear things up." My eyes drop from his stare to the elephant in the room. "There's some gossip going around. I'm afraid it will end up in the press."

"I could use the publicity," he answers swiftly, then slyly modifies it. "And the *show* could use the publicity."

I can't find the right way to tell him that the gossip is also about me because, well, a) I wish it were true and b) I am afraid it might spoil any chance of it becoming true.

"This is all about Mr. Darcy, am I right?" he asks.

I look away from the elephant and find myself nodding.

"He's being a selfish baby. All because of that wig! I don't have any problem talking about it to the press. I'm sure I can give them an earful. Let him try and sue me!"

My jaw would have dropped had it not already been hanging low but now I feel my eyes widening with fear, so I am grateful that Steve appears at the doorway and says, "Ten minutes to curtain," and ushers me out of the dressing room, closing the door behind me.

* * *

I watch the opening minutes of the show, appalled by the walking choreography that looks like the square dances I learned in grade school. The accents are horrendous because no one in the cast is British. No one in the production has bothered to hire a dialect coach or a choreographer because the director thinks he can do it all himself. As I slide out into the lobby, I see Barry talking with Gladys, the other co-producer, and the playwright. Gladys is on Nancy Lee's Sutton Place team, a wealthy lesbian who was born into the social register. She has a driver who drives her in her Mercedes from the East Side to the West Side to attend the performances. She is courting the actress who plays Elizabeth Bennet. Every evening they dine together after rehearsals or a performance. The playwright-composer, Susan Bridges, is a grade school teacher from Kentucky. She adapted the Jane Austen novel with simple tunes and dances for her students to perform, which caught the attention of the nearby regional theater which caught the attention of Gladys because she is a patron who regularly trolls their new play festival looking for hits for potential girlfriends.

Barry sees me and nods. Gladys gives me a look of dismissal, as if I am a servant who has wandered into the wrong wing of the house. The joke is on her. I am not sleeping with an actor in the show; I am sleeping with Barry, off and on since rehearsals began. It's sporadic because we both have to keep office hours and theater hours. And avoid Steve on the side. Barry is more than a decade older than Steve, which makes him considerably older than me. He's short and swarthy and full of passion. Theater. Dance. Money. Sex. In my bedroom, we tumble and grope and clutch and roll. It's a good workout for me since I cannot afford the membership to a gym.

Barry's net worth began with his grandfather, one of the New York banking barons who survived the depression, which is why he gets along so well with Gladys. I know that Barry and Gladys had dinner with Nancy Lee and her partner the evening before, because he showed up to my apartment afterward, failing to mention, however, that I was a source of gossip, possibly because he was the one gossiping about me, to keep himself legitimate and Steve off our scent. Gladys calls Steve every day wanting an update on the cast, mostly to make sure that the actress who is playing Lizzy is not acting with another actress. Gladys is clueless about Steve's rousings with Mr. Bingley. Barry, however, is aware of it, though it doesn't stir any jealousy on his part. He adores knowing that Steve is adored by others. I think if Gladys knew about Steve's backstage behavior, she would threaten to fire Steve, the same way that Nancy Lee has threatened me. It's okay for the dykes to play around, but when the faygelahs do, they consider it too dangerous.

Alan, the house manager, slides out of the theater doors and into the lobby. He approaches me and tells me that a certain starlet is in the house. She is pretty and blonde and buxomy and appeared in the high-grossing action movie that Mr. Darcy starred in. I mention that I didn't see her arrive, adding that I thought she had planned to attend the opening night of the show the following week. Barry overhears this and asks if we can alert photographers to show up backstage.

"Do you think you can talk him into taking a photo?" Barry asks me about the action hero attempting to impersonate a gentleman on stage, knowing, of course it is an impossible request and the reason why he wants to fire Nancy Lee.

I look at him and wonder why he is torturing me in public when we fit so comfortably together privately in bed. He, in fact, has also ridiculed Mr. Darcy's toupee. He and Gladys both want the action hero to be starring in the lackluster adaptation of Jane Austen's most popular novel, not the wig-wearing imitation. The playwright is the only obstacle preventing the high grossing shiny scalp from having a starring role on Broadway.

I walk outside into the drizzly cold air and the bright lights. I look up and down the block, walk around to Shubert Alley. The marquees twinkle and blink in the light rain. I am hoping that I spot one of the roving photographers who are often on the search for a big photo to sell to the papers. No such luck on this bone-chilling night.

When I return to the theater the lobby is empty. I cross the street to Charlie's, a restaurant and bar that always has a crowd of theater-working professionals. Sam, the maitre'd, asks me how's the house and I answer "fearful." At the bar I see Jack, an apprentice with the general management company, and Bryan, a friend who is also an apprentice publicist. I see that Gladys and Barry and the school teacher-playwright have taken a table in the back corner of the restaurant. I ask Bryan if he has his camera with him and if he wants to make some money later taking a backstage photo. He agrees. He'll get double paid if he can sell something to one of the newspapers.

I sit at the bar and order a drink and a burger. I have no money for either, but will have Sam charge it to Nancy Lee's house account at the restaurant. I think if I can get a good backstage photo my job will be safe and Barry will be pleased and I might even get a raise. I talk a few minutes with Jack because I have a crush on him. His boyfriend is the company manager of the hit musical playing next door to the travesty inspired by Jane Austen.

I look at my watch and walk over to the theater and watch the last minutes of the first act. It's a tedious display of square dancing. The singing is off-key. The end is greeted with tepid applause. As the house lights rise I meet the starlet at her seat and ask if she would like to come back stage for a photo afterward. She has bright white teeth and fake-blonde hair and distinct cleavage, whether or not it is real or fake. She agrees and I tell her I will meet her at the end of the show.

* * *

Backstage, I tell Steve about the surprise guest in the audience. I tap on Mr. Darcy's dressing room door and peer in. He is shirtless, sitting on a chair before a mirror, patting his face with a tissue. He sweats profusely. There have been as many meetings held on how to prevent the rivers of stains seeping through his costumes onstage as to the false hair he is wearing on his head. He requires two duplicate costumes for each act. A dresser stands in the wings and pats his sweat away or helps him undress and dress. She is matronly and indistinct and arouses nothing in no one, especially Mr. Darcy. I barely detect her in the room pressing a costume for the next act. As I look down at him I realize how good-looking Mr. Darcy is. His arms are thick and hairy, his chest is beautifully muscled and furred. I tell him about tonight's guest in the audience and that she would like to come backstage after the show.

"No photo," he says.

"I could give you time to change," I say, thinking that this would give him time to remove his toupee, believing, of course that he is probably more embarrassed by the wig than by the bad costumes and the sweating.

"No photo," he says again.

I nod and back out of the room as the matronly dresser flips over the costume and continues ironing.

I'm not a good actor so I know my disappointment registers on my face. In the hallway, the actor playing Mr. Collins stops me and asks me about the interview slip Nina has sent him. He wants to know what kind of talk show he has been booked on.

I say, "Cable. Good exposure." I don't say, however. "No pay. No audience. No ratings. And the host is a bona fide idiot."

I watch the second act from the back of the theater. More than half of the audience left after intermission. Even the freebies are gone. The actress playing Elizabeth Bennet is not the prettiest of sisters, but she is still miscast. She has no cleverness in her voice, every sentence sounds like it is one long, low note. She scowls or smiles, otherwise there is no wit in her manner, and she tromps around on stage like a brainless tomboy. In one of the dances an actor loses a shoe. In another, a dress snags and rips. All lyrics are unintelligible.

At the end of the show I meet the starlet at her seat and walk her and her date through the underground tunnel that leads backstage to the dressing rooms. Her date is a star on a daytime television soap opera, short and young, with beautiful black hair and a gorgeous smile. I know he's a plant to upstage Mr. Darcy.

As I walk them toward Mr. Darcy's dressing room, I waive Bryan through the backstage door.

The starlet and her date arrive at Mr. Darcy's dressing room before Bryan and I make it down the hall. Mr. Darcy sees us approaching and his face becomes red and angry. He slams his dressing room door closed.

I anticipated that this would happen. Bryan and I wait in the hallway, hoping we might catch a candid photo on the sly. A few minutes later the starlet and her date emerge through a thinly cracked door, as if they now know Mr. Darcy has no intention of being photographed. Her face is tense but her date is bemused. I smile as if nothing bad has transpired and offer to introduce them to the rest of the cast. Mr. Bingley's dressing room is the closest. As I knock on his door, I notice he has already decamped from the constrictions of his costume. The elephant is free. Bryan snaps the photo, capturing everyone's astonishment and glee.

* * *

The photo runs three columns wide in the next day's newspaper. The caption mentions Mr. Bingley's pride but does not show it. He appears only shirtless. Gladys is furious because the actress who plays Elizabeth Bennet is angry. The actress is angry because the men in the show are getting more attention in the press than the women. The women are being overlooked, subjected to prejudice because of the vanity of the men. The world's most important literary heroine is invisible. She threatens to quit the show and talk to the press about it. Then Mr. Darcy threatens to quit the show but of course he is not talking to anyone about it or anything else.

Barry phones Nancy Lee. A news crew wants to film backstage, specifically with Mr. Bingley. Nancy Lee makes several phone calls to make it happen, but the union rules override it and the stagehands will not agree to it. It causes a fight with Nina because it makes Nancy Lee look like she is not good at her job, which she really isn't. Nancy Lee spends her days nursing a hangover and tucking her curly hair beneath a cowboy hat. Nina fidgets with her diamond rings, diamond earrings, and diamond necklace, worrying that the office does not have enough clients to pay the bills.

That evening, I deliver the press lists to the box office. Backstage, Mr. Bingley waves me into his dressing room and closes the door. I think he is going to ask me to help with the elephant, or at least introduce us, but instead he asks about the starlet's date from the night before.

"He said he would recommend me to his agent," Mr. Bingley says. "Could you get me his number?"

"His agent's number?"

He gives me a look like I am a stupid fool, which sometimes I am, especially in the presence of large flopping appendices. "Yes, that too," he says.

That evening, Mr. Darcy performs without a hairpiece. The audience responds better but the playwright is in tears. She cannot imagine Mr. Darcy with a bald and shiny scalp. She can't bear Elizabeth Bennet's voice. She can't believe that Jane Austen would suffer through any of this.

The following morning, Gladys calls the office and tells Nancy Lee to reschedule the critics who were coming to the weekend performances. Barry calls next and tells Nancy Lee that a famous rock star is coming to the show that evening. He wants to meet Mr. Bingley backstage after the performance. I spend the day on the phone, rescheduling critics and scheduling photographers.

* * *

On the weekend the actresses appear in costume in Times Square for a publicity stunt. They do a dance from the show and hand out flyers for discount tickets. Mr. Darcy and Mr. Bingley are a no show because they were never invited in the first place. Nancy Lee has Gladys pose with the women in the cast. The lady columnist who is dating Jane Bennet talks with Nina about the show, pretending to know nothing about Gladys and the actress playing Lizzy.

My weekend is spent backstage, bringing more celebrities and photographers to Mr. Bingley's dressing room.

After the Sunday matinee, Barry and I share a taxi back to my apartment. We spend a few hours in my bed romping and napping. When he rises to leave, I mention Mr. Bingley's interest in the short, good-looking soap opera star.

"Are you surprised?" he asks.

"Of course not."

Barry mentions that he thinks Mr. Bingley will be a big star.

I take the opportunity to mention Steve's special attentions pre-performances. Barry is not phased about it, which means he has always known and approved of it.

"Gladys threatened to fire Steve when she heard," he says. "So I threatened to fire Nancy Lee."

"So why did you tell Nancy Lee it was me?"

"I didn't," he answers. "Gladys did."

"Gladys?"

"She wanted to fire Nancy Lee too. And you would give her a reason."

* * *

On the same night critics arrive to begin attending performances a closing notice is posted on the bulletin board by the stage door. Word spreads quickly backstage. The actresses cry and show more emotion in their dressing rooms than they do in front of the stage lights. I spend my time handing out press tickets in the lobby before the show and bringing celebrities backstage to meet a shirtless Mr. Bingley.

Two days later the opening night party is held in a ballroom of a hotel near the theater. It has been lavishly decorated as though it was Pemberley, Mr. Darcy's residence. Waiters and waitress have been hired and properly costumed. A small quartet plays period music. More money has been spent on the party than on the production. Many celebrities are in attendance. The playwright is grinning from ear to ear, thrilled by anyone and everyone who crosses her path. Mr. Bingley holds court at a table of celebrities. Mr. Darcy and his wife and his agent sit at another table looking like they have shown up to the wrong party. Mr. Darcy is polite to anyone who arrives to the table to congratulate him on his performance, but he does not wander the room or pose for any photographs. His wife spends a lot of her evening chatting and drinking with Gladys and Nina, which makes me think that she is a lesbian too, and, to me, confirms the rumors of Mr. Darcy's suspected homosexuality. While Mr. Bingley's beaus are no secret to anyone, Mr. Darcy has managed to keep his reputation intact. Everyone in the cast and crew still question what team he really performs on, or, perhaps, if he plays on both sides.

I leave the party and walk to a newsstand on 42nd Street, buying the first editions of newspapers as they are delivered by trucks. The reviews are not merely tepid, they are sour, bitter, and angry. No one appreciates a badly performed musical theater version of *Pride and Prejudice*. The destruction of a Jane Austen masterpiece. Mr. Darcy is called bow-legged and blunt. His bare scalp is distracting. Elizabeth Bennet is called butch and boring. Her voice is deeper than Mr. Darcy's. There is no chemistry, no romance, no wit, and certainly nothing to be proud about. Only Mr. Bingley and his elephant emerge unscathed. One male critic calls him "a rising star," true to Barry's prediction.

Back at the party I hide the newspapers beneath my jacket and catch Nancy Lee's eyes as I walk through the ballroom. I follow her to a corner of the room for an impromptu meeting with the advertising team and Gladys and Barry. There are no quotes to be found in any of the print reviews. The television reviews are even worse. One critic even mentions the fact that they were barred from filming scenes of the musical.

Nancy Lee suggests that an ad be done for praise the novel has garnered from generations of authors and readers. The head of the advertising team thinks it is a terrific idea, but when she runs the cost by Gladys and Barry, they shake their head with displeasure, tabling any further discussion on the show until the morning.

The meeting breaks up. I see many guests now reading newspapers. When Barry leans over Mr. Darcy's shoulder I look away from that table. I know he is explaining the reviews to him. Steve is hovering around Mr. Bingley and his appendage and its fans. I see Jack at the bar and ask where his boyfriend is. They had a fight and he wanted to stay behind. We talk about Mr. Bingley, Mr. Darcy, and Jack's boyfriend. Jack follows me into a restroom. We make out in a stall and take turns giving each other blow jobs. When I return to the party I see that Mr. Darcy and his wife have left. Mr. Bingley is talking to a waiter. Barry and Steve are nowhere to be found.

* * *

The next morning the phone rings constantly in the office, the second-night critics from the outlying suburban newspapers and radio stations cancel their review tickets. I spend hours cutting out the reviews and pasting them onto white typing paper. They are horrible upon horrible upon horrible.

Nina panics and begins calculating office expenses that have been paid for the show, yelling at Nancy Lee that she neglected to tell her how much she was spending and now they have spent too much. Around lunchtime Gladys rings, confirming that the show will close on Sunday. A few minutes later, she calls again to say that the remaining performances are cancelled too. Mr. Darcy will not go on. I call all of the critics who have not already canceled to tell them that the show has closed. I reach Steve on the phone at his apartment and he tells me that he and Barry are going to the country. By country, he means Barry's house in the Hamptons. Southampton to be exact.

At the end of the work day, Nancy Lee and Nina pull me into the back room for a private conversation. Nancy Lee tells me with the show closing they do not have enough clients to keep me employed. Nina hands me a check for a last week's salary and tells me to clean out my desk. I'm annoyed that they waited to tell me this at the end of the day of the end of a week. Before I leave, I hand Nina my office key.

In the following days, I file for unemployment, entertain an offer at another publicity office, working on a planned musical adaptation of *The Grapes of Wrath*. It would give me enough weeks to finish my apprenticeship and join the union. I read in the gossip columns that Mr. Bingley has landed a sitcom role and Mr. Darcy has fired his agent. Steve calls me a few days later when he is back from the Hamptons. Barry has stayed in the country. "He found a bartender to flirt with," Steve says, not knowing, of course, how wounded I am to hear this.

Steve asks if I want to go with him that evening to the men's bathhouse in Chelsea. I agree and meet him later. In the locker room of the bathhouse we undress and shower and part company, each on his own quest. I watch a porn film in one room and an orgy in another. On another floor, I wander the hallway, looking into the small rooms and at the bodies reclining on mats that are atop blocks of wood that resemble beds. There is one room where the buttocks of a man lying on his stomach catch my attention. As I look into the room, the man turns his face to me and smiles. It is a familiar, gorgeous smile. Just as the beautiful black hair is.

Only later will we talk about Mr. Darcy and Mr. Bingley. He tells me Mr. Bingley never called, though Mr. Darcy did. "He thinks there is a role for me in his new movie," he tells me. "He's so much sexier without that toupee, don't you think?"

Elvis at Three is an Angel to Me

"You could go as Dolly Parton," Mark says.

I smile at the thought of it and then shake my head "no." I have no desire to dress in drag, even for a Halloween dance. Mark is teaching me a complicated two-step dance in the area of our apartment in Chelsea between the kitchen and the bathroom, a space that is no bigger than a bath mat. Mark thinks I need to be more outgoing if I want to find a boyfriend. I moved in with Mark because I hated living with the lesbian couple in the Village apartment where I slept on a sofa bed. It was a six-story walk-up and the lesbians had taught their small dog, a Pekinese, to piss and poop on a sheet of newspaper that was placed on the floor not far from where I slept. In Mark's apartment I have my own "room," a walled off space outside his bedroom. Now I have a bed and a closet and a shelf that runs along one side of the bed which I can use as a desk. It makes me feel a little more like an adult since I am now in my thirties.

I also moved in with Mark because I am in love with him. We met in an accounting class. Mark was tired of low-paying data processing jobs and also inching toward thirty. I wanted a backup skill greater than typing. Mark doesn't like being alone, so we began meeting for dinner before class and going to the movies when he wasn't doing something with his boyfriend. One night after class, Mark asked me if I wanted to move in with him because his boyfriend was moving out. The boyfriend told Mark he had a new boyfriend. Mark knew about the lesbians and my unhappiness about the dog pooping on newspaper. I was hoping Mark might also feel about me the way I felt about him, but then he said, "I know a guy who can build a temporary wall so we can turn the large room into a bedroom." The guy was also an ex-boyfriend of Mark's. Now, after living with Mark for more than a year, my silent, frustrating lust is more tolerable than smelling dog shit.

As Mark twirls me around he presses his hand at the small of my back and I feel the wetness of my T-shirt against my skin. A pungent, yeasty smell encircles us. Mark sweats more than I do. In my opinion he perspires testosterone or whatever chemical lures insects into the mouth of a Venus Fly Trap, which is why it is so frustrating to be only Mark's friend and roommate. When my friend Billy first met Mark, he pulled me aside and asked, "Are you doing him?"

My eyes widened and I responded, "He has a boyfriend." Mark is seldom without a boyfriend, which he now defines to include his tricks and hook-ups and second-dates. "I'll never make that mistake again," Mark says about the boyfriend who moved out on him. "I'm not living with anyone again until I am certain about it." In many ways I hope he never meets that someone he is certain about, because it could mean I might win his love by default.

* * *

The Halloween dance is downtown and hosted by a group of expatriate Southerners. Halloween is a week away but on everyone's mind. I am dressed in bell-bottom jeans and a sailor's top that I found in the army/navy store on Christopher Street because money is tight and I have little confidence when it comes to flaunting my lack of a physique. The room is full of a lot of cowboys in boots and hats. There are a few guys in drag, though no one has showed up as Dolly Parton. Mark is dressed as Elvis. He is wearing a red satin jumpsuit opened to his navel with tuxedo stripes along the legs made of darker red sequins. He was able to go a week without shaving and now has appropriate muttonchop sideburns. In this crowd he is a standout, but Mark would be a standout even if he wasn't dressed as Elvis.

Before graduate school and working in data programming, Mark was a dance instructor. As a teenager, he flew to the resorts in Mexico and Miami, dancing his way into the winner's circle with several older women partners. Mark has a swimmer's physique, wide shoulders tapering to an impossibly thin waist. He likes to show off his biceps, though his dark chest hair and abdominal muscles are the star of his Elvis outfit.

Mark and I dance around the room to a fast two-step. I think we make a perfect couple. We're the same height, and in the blur of motion, I think I am as good looking as Mark. It's part of a ritual so everyone in the room knows Mark is the best dancer in the room and I am his inadequate partner. As we show off our new routine, I am altogether elated, thrilled, embarrassed, and deflated because it means I have Mark's friendship but will see little of him for the rest of the evening. When we finish, he dances with a tall fellow named Gus and I go to the table where there are drinks and order a beer, eyeing the handsome guy behind the counter.

I have a complicated backstory with the South. I was the only child of four who went to college. I left Georgia without coming out to my parents. I always hoped that I might one day return and introduce them to a perfect significant other, which would force them into accepting "my lifestyle choice," but just as that sort of happiness has eluded me, so has my failure to cash into a lucrative profession. In fact, after leaving several jobs that I felt demanded too much from me, I have started simplifying my life because I find other things more important. I type and temp and work in a kitchen that prepares meals for homebound clients with AIDS. I used to be a "buddy" to a guy who lived on the Upper East Side, which meant riding the subway for hours to take him to doctor appointments and buy his groceries. He was the third buddy in a row that I lost so I am taking a break until I am ready to have another buddy.

I see Mark dancing with the handsome guy who was working the bar and I am stung with jealousy and envy, even though lust and sex mix uneasily in my mind these days with uncertainty and fear. I leave the party early, walk home to the apartment, stopping at a donut shop on the corner. Back in my bedroom I devour the donut, picking off the sugar flakes from my T-shirt and tapping them against my tongue where they dissolve. Later that evening, I hear the thumping of boots as they land on the floor. Elvis has returned home with a new boyfriend.

* * *

A few weeks later, just before Thanksgiving, Mark asks me if I have dated anyone HIV-positive. It's a strange question because he knows I seldom have dates but not so strange since he knows I am now accompanying my friend Billy to doctor appointments. Billy and I dated briefly before we settled on being just friends. Before I can formulate a decent answer, Mark begins crying and says Ted called and told him he tested HIV-positive. Ted was the boyfriend who moved out before I moved in with Mark. Mark and Ted had lived together for almost a year, which in my mind provides enough explanation for Mark's tears. Mark has never been tested and isn't sure he wants to be tested. A question mark rattles around in his mind more and more because he doesn't like the uncertainty. That evening we watch a movie in my bedroom and Mark falls asleep beside me.

Uncertainty haunts my life. At first, Billy said the red blemish on his chin was a pimple that would not go away. One evening while we were in the lobby of a theater, he confessed he had tested positive. Now I know all of his medications. His family in New Jersey does not know he has been diagnosed with AIDS and he has no plans to tell them. I feel a pang of homesickness when he tells me about arguing with his mother. Money is tight this year and I cannot travel south for the holidays. I fight the shame of being different, a black sheep expatriate.

The following day, Billy has a blood transfusion. I stay with him in the hospital, trying to fall asleep in a chair. The next morning, we take a cab to his apartment. Before I leave, he asks me if I will move in with him. His roommate is only on a month-to-month arrangement. I'm surprised by the question. Billy knows how I feel about Mark. "You're the only one who knows what to do," Billy says.

I see in Billy's eyes his fear of being alone. "I don't mind staying over to help," I answer and that seems to calm him for now.

Mark is distraught when I return to the apartment. "Where were you?" he asks, in a tone that suggests I have abandoned him.

* * *

Mark returns to suburban Virginia for the holidays. Billy goes to suburban New Jersey for a few days. I deliver meals and talk to my family on the phone, pretending to be cheerful.

When Mark returns to the city, he says he wants to go to the dance on Saturday evening. Saturday morning the phone rings and Mark learns that his father has died of a heart attack.

"I think I can catch the next train," he says.

With one phone call I can see how his face has aged. He's no longer a boy in search of impromptu adventures. I want to offer him comfort but I stiffen because I don't want him to know how much I care for him.

It is a month before I see him again. One night when I return from Billy's apartment Mark is home. He tells me right away that he needs to take care of his mother and that he is moving out at the end of the month. He says he will speak to the landlord about having the lease put into my name.

That evening, Mark crawls into my bed. We watch TV, a science fiction movie I have rented.

Sometime in the night I roll over and hold him. He gasps and begins crying.

* * *

Thirty years later my father is recuperating from open heart surgery. A few months before, my mother passed away from Alzheimer's. I have returned to the South I left a lifetime ago to help my father. I am sleeping in my boyhood bedroom, though nothing of my life remains in the room. This is the room where my mother spent the last months of her life. The house seems odd without her. She is everywhere and nowhere. A year before her death when I visited my parents for the holidays, she told me I reminded her of her son Jimmy. I told her I was still her son Jimmy, only the older and fatter version of him. I said it as a joke, a light-hearted comment to smooth over her mistake. I saw the weight of my remark travel across her mind, in search of a memory.

"Did you get the candy?" my sister asks me on the phone. I am standing in the kitchen, checking the medications my father must take.

"What?"

"The candy? For the trick-or-treaters."

I had forgotten today was Halloween. In my mind it was only the end of the month when expenses are totaled, reconciliations are made, and the rent is mailed.

When a nurse arrives at the house, I jump into my rental car and buy candy from the nearby pharmacy, which is the size of my former high school's football field. On the drive I think about how everything in my life has changed and how memories make me weep.

"What time do they arrive?" I ask my father when I am back at the house.

"Who?" he asks.

"The trick-or-treaters."

I see his face change in the way my mother's did not long ago, searching for memories. "Oh, I don't think we'll get anyone," he says. "The kids are all grown up and moved on."

I lay the bowl of candy out by the front door and look out the window at the empty street. In our neighborhood there were always children playing and families outdoors. The Stewarts. The Turners. The Duncans. The Bradfords. As much as my parents wanted to keep our news from others, news happened and arrived. Alice Duncan committed suicide. Wes Turner was killed in a car accident. The Stewarts divorced. Craig Bradford was arrested for selling drugs. My crime was dual: being gay and leaving home for New York City.

I go into the kitchen and unload the dishwasher. The floor beneath the sink door is warped and creaks with my weight. In the next room my father listens to the news, the volume deafening.

A few minutes later I hear a ding-dong. It's a familiar-unfamiliar sound until I remember it is the sound of our doorbell. I walk to our front foyer and open the door to find a young boy of five dressed as a pirate. He has on a three-corner hat and an eye patch. He turns and waves to a younger child who holds the hand of a woman I take to be his mother, signaling that the coast is clear and candy is in sight. The younger brother toddles toward the door. I imagine he is about three years old. He is dressed in a red jumpsuit and has fake sideburns and is wearing rhinestone eyeglasses. Behind him and next to the woman, I see a smiling man I take to be his father.

For a split second I am thrown back in time. Mark Moore shows up like an apparition in my thoughts and my breathing stops. His mother buried him in the family plot in Virginia.

He was not yet thirty-three. I could not afford the trip south to attend his funeral.

The older brother waits until the younger boy is at the door and then looks up at me and says, "Trick or treat!" His younger brother gives a faint giggle and sputters out the same sound.

I let them take all the candy they want, studying the younger brother too closely as if an angel has appeared out of a mist, and then wave to the parents as if they were my friends as the brothers run across our lawn.

Behind the closed door, I run through a list of names I refuse to forget. Jordan, Peter, Dave, Billy, Mark.

How to Obtain
an Alfred Hitchcock Physique
(and Bonus Dark Psyche)

1. Wait until you reach your late thirties when you are at the peak of your beauty. More handsome than you will ever be again. Fall in love with a married man. A decade older with a wife and two kids who live in the suburbs. Make sure he is wealthier than you, which could be any man in the city, since you are a fiction writer working as a temporary employee at a computer terminal in a corporate office making a sub-poverty wage. Overlook, at least for the moment, that you have a twenty-nine inch waist.

2. Make sure the married man is tall, attractive, and sought after by both men and women. Be sure he has a roving eye, which shouldn't be difficult, since most men working or living in the city have a roving eye, whether they are secretly gay or openly out. Pretend, however, you do not see the wandering eye and it does not exist. Love does not come to you often and you don't want to blow your chances that the older married man might love you as much as you will love him.

3. Accept all of his invitations for dinner, for plays and musicals, for movies, for trips to the Hamptons and Palm Springs and Fort Lauderdale. Feed into his narcissism and vanity. Compliment him on his new shirt, his new haircut, his

new sports car. Wear the Speedo or briefs he likes you to wear. Do everything he wants to do in bed and then some. Make sure his desire to seek pleasure is exhausted.

4. Learn to appreciate fine cuisine and expensive cocktails, especially cocktails. Remember to smile and be non-confrontational. Pretend you are a character in a musical comedy, the one who sings the funny song and tap dances and the audience falls in love with.

5. Compare your shabby, west-side Hell's Kitchen rent-stabilized fifth-floor walk-up to his luxury Upper East Side duplex with a balcony and a doorman. This is a crucial step in developing your soon-to-be dark psyche. Spend as much time with him as he wants you to spend with him and then make him think about you when you are not there. Leave behind in his apartment your briefs, socks, T-shirts, razor, and toothbrush so you know there will always be a next time.

6. Make sure he is a goal you wish to achieve. Since you can't afford to take him out to dinner, offer to cook for him in his kitchen. Make him Belgian waffles for breakfast. Cornish hens for dinner. Spice the coffee with bourbon and keep the wine flowing. After eating, have sex in front of the picture window of his balcony so that everyone in eyesight will see that you mean business. Smile when he tells you he is filing for divorce. Wake him up in the middle of the night for more sex. And again before he gets up in the morning.

7. Ignore the comment your best friend makes: "If he cheats on his wife, he will cheat on you."

8. Fake a smile when he tells you he loves money more than sex. Do not feel wounded when he says, "I wish you made more money." Learning how to deflect your emotions will make you a more better and more bitter person.

9. Tell him he doesn't have to do something special for your fortieth birthday so you know he will.

10. Agree to frequent flyer miles to Paris. Accept aging by candlelight.

11. Say yes when he asks you to move in with him. Explain to your friends you are giving up your rent-stabilized apartment because you are finally in love. Ignore their horrified stares. Do not hear their pleas, "Why not sublet?"

12. When, on moving day, he gives you a set of keys and tells you not to use this address for any mail because you are not on the lease, do not look fazed. Do not show your concern when he says you must have your own phone line installed because you cannot answer his phone. Overlook your fear of potential homelessness and danger. It will surface again later.

13. Rearrange your life to revolve around him. Cook. Clean. Engage in sex. Tell yourself cohabitation does not mean giving up your independence. Show up late at your temp job because you need time to spend alone at the gym. Breathe a sigh of relief when he unexpectedly goes out of town on business.

14. Ignore the crumbled yellow post-its you see in the trash can in the kitchen with names of men and their personal phone numbers. Do not listen to the message on his answering machine placed on the side table on his side of the bed from a man with a deep whispery voice asking if they can get together again. The message will nonetheless be burned into your memory.

15. Look through his daybook and convince yourself all the names and numbers are business associates, even though a few will match those on the post-its you have saved from the trash.

16. Consider your options. An open relationship. Experimentation. Three-ways. Orgies. Confrontation. Potential homelessness and danger.

17. Tilt your head with concern when he tells you his ex-wife wants half his money. Listen to him rant about her robbing him of his hard-earned cash. Silently imagine how she must feel. Him cheating on her for years and years and years, only discovering now that he is gay.

18. Feel worthless when he tells you one morning that you need to contribute more money to his lifestyle. Worry about helping him maintain this luxury. Develop your darkening psyche by practicing mumbling so you cannot be understood.

19. Work double shifts. Engage in less sex with him. Skip making him dinner. Show up late to the apartment one evening reeking of cigarette smoke and climb into bed without saying anything to him. When he asks you where you were, tell him you went out with friends. Make sure he doesn't believe you by giving him the smirk you have secretly practiced for months.

20. Believe things get better. Have more fights about money. Refuse to fly to Las Vegas because you can't afford your share of the fare. Forgive him when he says he is sorry. Have sex to feel happy again. Return to cooking for him, sneaking portions for yourself while he is out of the room. When he asks you one night why you didn't make a salad and you cannot tell him because you had no money left for grocery shopping, stare at the knife in your hand a little too long for comfort. Realize that there are weapons all around the kitchen. Forks. Pans. The Belgian Waffle Maker.

21. Place the knife in the sink but continue thinking about it. Look for weapons to use in the dining room. The bathroom. And the bedroom. Imagine holding the weapons, making them levitate and spin like you possess the psychokinesis of

a disturbed teenage girl. Wonder what mental link separates you from a murderer. What will it be that will finally make you snap? Make the weapons fly across the room to their target.

22. After sex, revisit the image of the knife. Think about the consequences. The blood. The police. The repercussions with family, friends, co-workers. You imagine an alternate life. Behind bars. On trial. Wonder what a boyfriend in prison might be like. Wonder what kind of tattoos you might get. Spend time thinking of obscure Latin phrases to have your new boyfriend carve into your flesh.

23. Ignore the strain in your expression when you shave in the morning. Do not cry when he tells you at breakfast that he wants an open relationship. Do not disagree when he suggests during dinner you move out.

24. Find an apartment in midtown, West Side, near the tunnel, rent-stabilized. Feel relief about regaining your independence, but fret about paying higher rent. Practice fighting anger and depression in front of your new bathroom mirror. Try not to place blame but place blame everywhere, especially on him. Drink more, eat less, then eat more and drink more. This is an important step in developing your new physique.

25. Ignore his phone calls and messages until you can't ignore them anymore. Meet for make-up sex and break-up sex several times. Spend a weekend in Key West with him. Make him pay for everything. Plane tickets, hotel, food and booze. Be sure to over eat and over drink. Then decide to never see him again.

26. Compare him to your other lovers, living and dead. Tricks. Boyfriends. Friends. Co-workers. Convince yourself he falls short in every category. Think about revenge. Imagine committing a crime without remorse. Practice psychokinesis. Wonder what the ex-wife must be feeling.

27. Cook yourself elaborate meals. Drink lots of cheap wine. Watch movies about serial killers. Criminals on the run. Become fascinated with sex crimes. The characters. The situation. The motive. The psychology.

28. Reboot your creative streak. Write a ghost story about a former lover. Write a novel about a recent crime. Learn more about how people think and tick. Double down deep on desire and what it makes people do. Never forget that you were once razor close to being a serial killer with psychokinesis.

29. Survive a terrorist attack, a hurricane, a bout with shingles, and your gym going out of business. Ignore your expanding waist, except when you need to shop for new pants.

30. Buy a contraption that electrocutes the rats in your apartment. Drop them in the garbage cans outside your building. When the pipes freeze and burst in your bathroom, watch your favorite books float in the ice cold water. Continue to blame him for all of this because of the apartment you had to give up. Some days, give into the rage. Send the knives flying into potatoes and bread and the chunks of ice that haunt your freezer.

31. Stop dating when it feels like work. Stop picking up men for sex when one steals your watch.

32. Accept a full-time job with benefits and overtime and responsibility. Settle into your forties. Pay off your debt. Enroll in a 401(k) plan. Learn to go to bars to drink, not to cruise. Keep tabs on crimes committed by younger men. Especially gay-for-pay porn stars. And married men fooling around on their wives.

33. Ignore your receding hairline, ignore your hair turning gray. Ignore the loss of muscle tone and dryness of your skin.

34. Overlook the fact that you have become invisible to other gay men, because you have become more visible to your friends. They love your bitterness. They love your tales of imaginary revenge. Everyone wants to have dinner with you because you can make them laugh with stories about levitating knives.

35. Forget to weigh yourself in the mornings. Always order the fries instead of a salad. Never go to sleep on an empty stomach. Enjoy your crazy, far-out dreams.

36. Accept an invitation to attend a friend's wedding. A few days before, realize you have had so many dinners you have no clothes that fit. Shop for a blue blazer then decide on a black one because it will match your black pants. Pick out a white shirt and a skinny black tie.

37. Smile when a friend snaps your photo with his cellphone at the wedding. Frown when he shows you the picture. Your waist is wide. The tie is too skinny. It makes your physique looks like a ski jump. Suppress your desire for revenge by remarking that you have turned into Alfred Hitchcock. It makes him laugh, so you laugh along with him, at yourself.

38. Fret about the photo during the reception. Drink too much so that your psychokinesis returns. Watch the happy, newly married couple cut the cake with an extraordinary large knife. Think about this knife. Tables full of weapons of cutlery and glass. Think about revenge and mayhem and lots of blood. Eat a second piece of cake.

39. Back in your apartment, fight off depression by looking at yourself in the mirror, convincing yourself that what you see is not what others do. Welcome in solitude. One day wake up and look in the mirror, pout your lips, and affect a British accent. You speak to your image: "Good evening, ladies and gentlemen." It makes you laugh. Like the time when you were

a kid and wore fat wax lips. Only now your imaginary monster is the real you.

40. Ignore time passing. Overlook the further expanding waist. Pretend the jowls make you look handsome.

41. Sometime in your early fifties, your ex-boyfriend writes you an email. On the morning you discover it, consider deleting it unread, but wait. Enjoy your bitterness.

42. Pace back and forth in your tiny apartment. Fret about the email. Worry that something has happened to him.

43. Contemplate your waist and the knife and the psychokinesis.

44. When you finally open his email, you see he sent it to you at four a.m. Imagine him drunk, lying in his bed in his Upper East Side luxury apartment with his laptop open. Lonely. Stood up. Robbed. His message is only two words. "Any regrets?"

45. Spend the rest of the day crafting a response. Make sure you don't delay, otherwise you would look dismissive. Unconcerned about him.

46. Fall asleep without responding because all of the bitterness and thinking leaves you exhausted.

47. Finally, wake up at four a.m. and type a response back to him, making sure it responds only to the two words he wrote that were followed with a question mark. "Any regrets?"

48. Type: "I regret losing my waist. But I had a lot of fun watching it disappear."

49. Click send.

50. Go back to sleep.

My Adventure with Tom Sawyer

One of the best dates I ever had was not a date at all, or at least that was the way Evan reacted to it when I had described my experience to him a few weeks after the fact. "Sounds like he was a cock tease," Evan said.

"No," I answered. "He was very sweet about everything."

The truth of the matter was that I had experienced a bad buildup before the great-date-that-was-not-really-a-date happened, which may have exaggerated my rating of it into the stratosphere. I had spent the prior year watching my love life turn me, literally, into the one of the Great Walking Wounded. After breaking up with Tony I fought off a case of shingles; I went through two root canals while I was trying to decide whether or not to continue seeing Bernie after three months, and when the six-week relationship with Hal failed to go any further so did I, stumbling down a flight of steps and tearing a ligament in my foot which required a set of crutches for me to use in order to be mobile.

That was when Evan suggested I get out of town and do some healing. "Use the cabin," he said, referring to a small rural property he owned with his significant other. "We're not going up there again till next month."

It sounded like a plausible idea, even with crutches—to be isolated in the upstate woods without a guy anywhere in sight whom I could conceivably want to date, with no TV to watch and a bag of books to read, so Evan dropped off the cabin keys to my apartment and I crawled aboard a bus and slept through the ride to the country. A few hours later, I was standing in a small, rural village wondering what I could possibly have been thinking of by leaving behind my brand new air-conditioner and round-the-clock support structure in the city. The taxicab I had called was not really a taxi nor a cab when it stopped in front of me to take me the next seven miles to the cabin, but the passenger seat in the front of an old red pickup truck, and the driver was not a fully-licensed or registered or official or professional taxi driver either, but a boy, a nineteen-year-old boy with floppy golden hair, ice blue eyes, an impossibly thin waist, and the most beautiful set of arms that a slender young man could possess.

"My uncle's tied up at Mrs. Smith's farm," the young one said to me when he announced that he could be the only way I would get to my final destination. "You don't mind, do you? I can get you there in this."

Of course I was immediately suspicious—that was my urban reflex system cracking into high gear—and just as I was about to ask his age I felt too old and vulnerable to move my mouth, standing there with my crutches and my suitcase of books, not able to take my eyes off of young Tom Sawyer's impossibly beautiful physique, and I was aware that I was having one of those awful motion picture moments when the old-maid spinster realizes her tour guide is someone generations younger than she is. Or worse, finding myself in a country-music version of *Death in Venice*.

(Did I mention that young Tom's shirt was sleeveless and unbuttoned in the front and that the jeans he wore were cutoffs because it was summer and it was hot? Should I mention that he had a baseball cap stuck in the back of the cut-offs and that even with that slight bulge in the pocket that the hat created it was unable to ruin the bubble shape of his ass? Would you believe me if I said the young man's complexion was pale and creamy except where it was red at the cheeks and slight washed with freckles across the bridge of his nose and that his teeth were remarkably even and white, or is that taking the image too far?)

So hobble and humble I did, right into the front seat of his truck.

His name was Scott and his truck was a year older than he was. He was twenty. Almost. That meant he was still in his teens—nineteen, a teenager—and his truck was built the year I graduated college. I was old enough to be his father. I found this out as Scott drove and pointed out the local landmarks worth noting (the new Laundromat where the dryers took dollar bills, the green-painted barn on the property which had once been a women's commune, and the small stream and the new stone bridge where a wooden covered bridge had once stood until a fire had destroyed it three years before). I was reluctant about confessing too much about myself (sweep the dirt under the rug, just like everyone in my family had always done), so I kept him talking about himself as much as I could: he had been laid off from his job on the assembly line at the window factory, the bad job market had meant cobbling together a series of odd jobs instead, such as helping his brother do landscaping work and filling in for his uncle with the car service. He managed to work in a few questions of me, too, asking where I lived in the city and how I had broken my foot. (Like a stupid old fool, I wanted to tell him: running after some guy who was running after someone else.)

As we drove up a mountainside, down into a valley and through a forest, he asked how long I was staying at the cabin where we were headed. I answered a little less than a week, then found myself confessing my concerns of the wilderness around me like a true (and worried) cynical cosmopolitan: Were there bears and mice and snakes and mosquitoes and such out here? (Well, yeah, yeah, yeah, and uh, yeah!) Was I likely to encounter them at the cabin? (I think so. Maybe not all at the same time!) Would they play loud music like my upstairs neighbor and keep me up all night? (Ah-huh. That sounds like my brother!)

He mentioned his girlfriend's family was having a tough time with raccoons. ("Raccoons!" I said. "Don't they have rabies?") I tried not to let the information about there being a girl off-stage leave me too discouraged. Wasn't I here, in the country, to get away from men just like him? Those young, drop-dead gorgeous things I saw all the time in the city, walking from an audition to a photo shoot to a gallery opening to a sex club. Wasn't this sojourn of mine a time to repair, heal the damaged and maligned parts of me that had turned me bitter longer than this young man had been alive? I hardly imagined I would see this boyish thing again once this ride was completed. He was certain to be off to another paying customer and I couldn't even keep a boyfriend a decade older than me interested for more than six weeks, let alone a young one who was charging me by the inch.

The cabin was exactly as Evan had described it. Down a bumpy path that was part gravel, part dirt, made from pre-fab wood sections, with a tiny front porch and a chimney, the whole building smaller than my Manhattan apartment. I looked at it and thought, oh my, God, what have I gotten myself into? Scott helped me carry my bag of books inside and when I handed him his fare, plus a too generous tip because of his youthful beauty, he handed me a business card and said, "Call us if you need anything else—To check out bear tracks. Go down to village for supplies. Whatever."

Us, I noted him saying. Not *him*. Don't call me. Call *us*. I nodded as he left and was suddenly so worried that there was no food in the cabin that I forgot to give him a smile and a polite good-bye. Evan had not told me if there was any food in the place, nor what I would have to do if I needed to find food. I quickly discovered some canned soup in a cabinet, but could not spot a can-opener, then realized, when I turned on the faucet and the water appeared brown, that I was not about to stay here in this God-forsaken place unless, well, unless I could at least believe that the water was decent enough to drink.

I tried to relax for a few minutes, unpack, settle in, and start a book, but my mind was consumed that there was no satisfactory drinking water. As I read, my throat became drier and drier as words raced in front of my eyes and straight out my ears. Why had I not thought this trip completely through? Why hadn't Evan told me I needed water, of all things? And food and toilet paper and a can opener if I wanted to survive? Finally, feeling as if I had been dumped in the Sahara, I went to the phone and dialed the "Us" number on the card Scott had left. When a woman finally answered (after about the six hundredth ring), I explained my predicament and asked if someone could find me—wherever the hell in the middle of nowhere I was—and take me to a store.

By now I was sweating. It was hot outside and even hotter inside the cabin, and I felt all my body fluid flowing right through my pores. It was another ninety-minutes of sheer, dry torture before there was a knock at the door, because I was certain the woman who had taken my call was purposely trying to scare the High-Strung Undesirable I had become right back to the city where I came from. "Hey," Scott said, when I opened the door. "My mom said something happened."

I could not contain my embarrassment, felt my face redden and my throat constrict and the Mojave sand my tongue had turned into made my eyes go teary, ready to expel the last of my body's moisture. "I need to go to the store," I said rather curtly, then tried to find a way to soften my behavior, so I reached out for my crutch and hopped across the room.

"Sure," he said, and started out to his truck.

He helped me shop, following me patiently through the aisles of the tiny grocery store in town. The prices were astonishingly low, compared to my corner bodega in the city, though some of the items on the shelf seemed to be older than my driving-aide. Scott seemed to be a practiced companion, not wandering away, not trying to convince me to buy something I didn't want, no signs of boredom, and my first instinct was to turn to him and ask him to marry me because he was so much more composed than any guy I had dated in the last decade and gone shopping with, but then I realized I would not be able to fight off his potentially angry, insulted youthful fists with a crutch and my unbalanced posture once he realized what I really hoped and desired of him.

His gentlemanly behavior continued even when mine did not. (I had a snippy exchange with a clerk in the meat aisle when I couldn't see where they had stamped the expiration dates on the labels.) Scott carried the bags to the truck, helped me up into the passenger seat, even carried the bags into the cabin and emptied the contents onto the counter.

When I handed him his fare and another nice tip, I asked him if he wanted to stay for something to eat. Outside, the sun was setting, though it would be another good hour before it was fully dark.

He fumbled and squirmed at my unexpected invitation and said that he'd like to, but couldn't, he had promised his mother he would be home for dinner and then there was a few things he needed to talk to his girlfriend about. *Mother. Girlfriend*— these were such strange words to me that I almost asked for a definition or explanation of the terms. I really didn't expect he would take me up on my offer, but I also didn't expect he would have one of his own. As he was walking back to his truck, his head cast down toward the ground in thought, he stopped and yelled back to me and asked if I liked to go boating.

"Boating?" I echoed back at him, not really understanding the concept of a structure floating in water—we were in a forest, of all places—I knew of no lake nearby. So I thought he might have said, "Voting." "Do I like voting?"

"Yes, well, sure," I said, not wanting to displease him. I tried to sound positive and optimistic, and, well, *happy*.

Then he explained that he owned a small boat at a lake that was not far from my cabin and he needed to check up on it sometime the following day, and did I want to ride over with him to the lake—get out of the cabin for a while—and if the weather was good, we could go out for a bit on the lake.

I hung on to the *"we." "We could go out a bit."*

"Sure," I said, not at all worried that I was a hundred years old and had only one working leg. I closed the door dizzy and confused. Tom Sawyer had offered to take me out on his raft.

* * *

I waited and waited and waited and waited for young Tom Sawyer to show up the next morning. He called me early and said he had to run an errand for his brother, then called and said he needed to sub for his uncle for a fare in town, and then called and said he would have to drop his mother off at the church and would be over after that. It was after lunchtime when he finally showed up at the cabin, honking his truck from the end of the drive. "You ready?" he yelled out of the window, as if I had been holding him up. From the doorway I stood amazed at the impatience in his voice and I almost called out and canceled, till I noticed his smile, his too-white, beautiful nineteen-year-old smile. "Just a sec," I yelled back, hopped to my crutch and was out the door as quick as my one old reliable leg could take me.

"It's not far," he said, when I was settled in my seat and we were headed down the small road that led to the cabin. Not far turned out to be farther than you'd think. About an hour later we reached an enormous lake where there was a small inlet where ten boats were harbored. Scott pointed out the boat that was his, then sprang out of the truck and began unloading several bags from the back onto the dock. I hobbled over to the boat, waited for him to help me in, and then when he did, he began to toss the bags into the boat for me to catch. I tried to pretend that I was much stronger and sea-worthy than I really was, but each time I absorbed the weight of a bag, I felt my bum foot creak and burn with pain. Finally, when the last of the bags were inside the boat, Scott began pitching them into the hold.

The boat was a small sailboat, about twenty feet in length, named "The Harbor Witch," which I felt was an adequate description of my mood as I tried to catch my breath and keep steady. As Scott stood in the hold unloading the bags—canned foods, bottled sodas, towels, pillows, stuff like that—I stood at the doorway and watched. "It doesn't really belong to me," he said. "My brother said if I cleaned it up, I could take it out today."

At last there it was. The catch. The glitch. It wasn't Scott's boat, it was his older brother's and he was only allowed to use it if he cleaned it up for him. "What could I possibly do?" I asked, leaning into my crutch and balancing myself as the boat wobbled in the water. I didn't expect that he would take me up on my half-hearted offer. First of all there was the crutch, which I clutched for dear life as the boat pitched back and forth. Then there was the fact that I was a guest. An invited guest. You don't ask invited guests to clean your brother's boat. Do you?

But he did. "Mop, I guess," he said.

Mop? He wanted me to mop? I don't think I actually articulated my exasperation, but it must have shown through in my tense, cynical, horrified urban personality and posture. Then I realized that if I stormed away in a huff I was a good hour's way from the cabin with no way to get back unless I called a cab. *Him.* I would have to call him.

"Or scrub if it's easier for you."

Scrub? If it's easier?

And then there was the smile. (And I suppose I should add that he was dressed in shorts and a tank-top, his shoulders smooth and deeply muscled, with the silky blond hair of his armpits peeking out beneath them.) Yes, he *was* Tom Sawyer. That smile had made me impossible to resist him. He soon had me starboard on my knees washing down his brother's boat, the sun beating against the back of my neck, the cool air from the water chilling the sweat of the T-shirt I wore and that I refused to take off because I was too worried it would reveal the layers of fat around my waist. Scott, however, took off his tank top, and I had chance enough to stretch and look and stretch and look and stretch and look. It was a glorious thing, really, working, stopping, looking at a young god sweat underneath the summer sun.

"Don't forget to clean the grommets," he said to me.

"Uh-huh," I answered. *Of course not. Don't forget the grommets.* Wasn't there a term for this sort of role playing I was willingly participating in. Slave/master? Sado masochism?

We mopped and cleaned and polished and when I thought we were almost done, Scott said there was "just a little more to do." Just a little bit more turned into another thirty minutes or so, but it was such simple, honest work, cleaning, sweating, and watching a beautiful young man, that I could not stop when he said we were through. In fact, I told him he had missed a spot where he had been polishing a rail and I went over and cleaned it up myself.

It was late afternoon when he showed me how to rig the sails and he used the small outboard motor at the back of the boat to guide us out of the harbor. When we were far enough out in the lake, he cut the engine and the sails caught the wind. He seemed to know what he was doing, yelling to me to watch the boom, demonstrating how to tie a proper knot and guide the rudder. Of course he made me wear a life jacket, which both upset and delighted me. It showed he cared enough if I were to drown, but there I was, next to a shirtless sailor at the helm of a sleek vessel, inflated and bulky like a bright orange rubber duck that would not sink.

As we sailed along the lake, Scott pointed out his favorite homes on shore, the one with the best pier, another which he felt certain was big enough to turn into a night club. We dropped anchor in a small cove and The Young Worthy Seaman asked if I wanted to take a swim to cool off. Yes, I thought, of course I do. I need to cool off. I've had more excitement today than I've had in the last twenty years. And I wanted to swim and frolic with the Beautiful Boy of the Lake no matter how much I resembled The Ugliest And Most Awkward Pool Toy in the Store. While Scott was in the galley doing something or other, I took off the lifejacket, took off my T-shirt and shorts, unwrapped the bandage from my leg, wrapped a towel around my waist to retain my modesty (and my growing desire) and put the lifejacket back on. Scott helped me to bow of the boat and we momentarily discussed the best way for me to jump into the water, whether it would hurt my leg less to fall on my good side or go straight in. He was now wearing nothing—having shed his shorts (like I did) and I could not keep my concentration focused on How to Jump when there it was, The Thing That Made Him So Young and Desirable, right there, right there beside me and in full glorious view. (And yes, he was hung, exactly as you'd expect a nineteen year-old guy to be—a large, heavy set of balls and a pink, fleshy sausage of a cock.) Finally, I was so agitated and hot, hot, hot, that I just dropped my towel and fell overboard into the water. It was a glorious, wonderful and cooling dunk and Scott dove in as soon as he saw me bob to the surface.

Scott swam and dove beneath the water, circling the Great Orange Inflatable Head I was now, talking about this and that as he gulped for breath and tossed the water out of his hair. "This is my favorite spot," he said and I cast my eyes around the lake and the shoreline as if we were pirates who had landed and found buried treasure. "Cindy—my girlfriend—doesn't like the boat at all. She thinks it's too much work. She'd rather have a speed boat. My brother says she just doesn't get it. Sailing. You know all the work and lessons to feel the wind catch in the sail and carry you away. Without the motor."

I nodded and bobbed and smiled in the best way I knew. At that moment I felt happy and content; the sun was glowing orange, setting slowly in the sky, the water was warm and still around us, broken only by Scott's swimming and splashing. In the water I could move and kick my foot, whereas on land I felt useless. And for a moment I had left behind my daily urban struggles and continual boyfriend troubles—I expected nothing from Scott—certainly nothing in the romance or sexual department—other than one nice surprise after the next. Which was exactly what happened.

"I wish I didn't have to go back," he said. "Don't you ever wish that? That you didn't have to go back to something that you don't like when you're somewhere that you're having a great time. Everyone's hocking me to keep applying for a job here or a job there. I just feel like I'm groveling. I want to do something I like to do and get paid for it."

"It's not easy putting yourself out there and asking for work," I said. I thought about all the jobs I had waded through in the last few years—from a publicist to a temporary office assistant to a newspaper editor to an occasional bartender until I landed in the communications office at the corporation where I had a steady position. "I'm sure you'll find a job soon. Just keep asking everyone you know. Someday somebody will hear of something. That's usually how it works. Somebody heard of something and remembered you were looking for a job."

"But I hope I like it," he said. "That's got to be important. I want to do it. Why can't I have a job doing something like this?"

"No reason why you can't," I said. "But that means you have to really look for it. You can't wait for it to come along."

The sun was now a bright orange ball floating on the surface of the water. I imagined myself falling in love with a boy less than half my age and it was a glorious fantasy. And for a moment I wasn't the older man. I was as young and beautiful and as eager as him. Ready to find and conquer the world.

"You know how to find the way back in the dark?" I asked. It wasn't really an overwhelming concern, just a thought that had emerged from the back of my mind as I looked at the setting sun. We had stayed out later on the lake than I had expected.

"I don't have to be back till morning," he said.

That was when it struck me that we weren't rushing back so quickly. He realized his mistake immediately—of not telling me his plans for fear of my casting doubt or suspicion on them. He floundered a moment by scrunching up his face, then said, "I can take you back if you want. The boat's real comfortable though. Or we can sleep up there. I've done it before. It's real neat. Feels like you're right under the stars."

Sleep on the boat? Or outside in the wilderness? What was he thinking? Who did he think I was? Davy Crockett? I looked at the boat and then at the shore. "Okay," I said in a weakened voice. Who was I to spoil the adventure?

* * *

We decided to camp on shore. Scott got cushions from the boat and we floated out various things to dry land—a blanket, towels, frying pan, canned foods, beer, matches. On shore, he spread out the blanket and I collected sticks and twigs, and we started a small fire at a spot enclosed by stones (where someone had obviously camped before).

We ate and drank the beers and sat beneath the stars and talked. I had dressed again in my T-shirt and shorts and re-wrapped my leg, but Scott sat shirtless, wearing only a towel around his waist, as if he were a native tribesman entertaining the Great Big Fat Tourist. He confessed that he'd had an argument with his girlfriend the day before; it had happened right before he had picked me up at the train station and had continued with her throughout the day. He said she was wearing him down, pressuring him to set a date for a wedding when he knew he wasn't ready or able to commit to her yet.

"She's not the right one," he said. "But I just can't tell her that. I'm too chicken. I don't want to start her crying."

Of course, I realized exactly how the girlfriend must be feeling, loving a god-like creature like this, unable to fully snare him and make him submissive. I started thinking about all the men whom I had dated who were really boys at heart, emotionally distant, romantically immature, especially the ones who thought the notion of a great date with me was going to a bar and looking at *other* guys.

"How come you don't have a girlfriend?" Scott asked.

It was a quick and hypothetical question, I knew that, but my stunned silence seemed to answer part of his question, so he backtracked and amended it with, "Or a guy? A boyfriend?"

I tried not to let my memories make me feel sorry for myself. "There was someone years ago," I said. "But he died. I just haven't found anyone else who seemed right. Right for me."

"My brother says I'll know when she's right," Scott said. "He says it'll just hit you in the heart."

"Is he married?" I asked.

"Divorced," Scott said. "He said he made a big mistake marrying Melinda."

We talked about other things—favorite movies, worst TV shows, places we wanted to visit, as the night fell deeper around us—crickets chirping, the wind rustling the leaves behind us, the fire snapping and talking as if it were another friend offering advice. We laid back on the blanket and looked at the sky and fell into a conversation about the possibility of God and our wish that He could provide us with more obvious and specific clues on how to live best.

Days later Evan asked me why I didn't just reach out and pounce on Scott and I tried to explain to him that it wasn't the most pressing desire of the moment, or, that, of course, it *was* the most pressing desire of the moment but that doing it, having sex—or trying to engage Scott in the possibility of sex with me—would have spoiled what was already there—a lush, romantic, sensual moment where nature displays every obvious and specific way you have been blessed.

I didn't tell Evan that I slept fitfully on the blanket, however, that I fell into one dream after the next, thinking that Scott was reaching out to me, embracing me, his lips pressing mine open and his body and hands finding every part of me I wanted him to find. I dreamed and dreamed and dreamed that he had moved closer, so much so that when I woke in the morning I was exhausted and hiding an erection that would not subside until the startling cold water of the lake forced it to disappear. I felt like a foggy old fool trying to keep up with Scott as we floated our things back to the boat, my throat dry, my breath stinking, what hair I still maintained spiking up in patches. Scott was unusually uneasy that next morning, as if he had made a mistake in camping out and now he was running late and he would soon be in big-time trouble with someone, and we used to the motor to sail the boat back to the harbor faster.

The ride back in the truck to the cabin was quiet and respectful, but I soon began wondering if my dreams the night before had been dreams at all, and that maybe Scott had really reached out to me sometime during the night and was now feeling sheepish of his behavior. I tried and tried to consider if it was a dream or of it were fact or if it were merely an old man's drunken memory of another lover of another time. At the cabin I invited Scott inside for breakfast or coffee or anything he wanted or needed, but he gracefully declined everything I offered and drove away, leaving me propped up on my crutches in front of the door. For the rest of the day I slept as much as I could, lifting myself back into the dream of Scott as often as possible, remembering the way he smelled and tasted and felt in my arms—or at least as I had imagined him to be. After a few hours of more sleep and dreaming, I masturbated myself awake and that seemed to break the spell, I had gotten him (somewhat) out of my system and was ready to move on.

I spent the rest of my time at the cabin reading the bag of books I had brought, some worthwhile, others not so. The first day or so I hoped Scott might call again and then I thought about calling him, but I knew that it was not the right thing to do—to engage myself further in such an impossible flirtation. On my final day, I packed and called the car service to take me back to the train station. Scott's mother said someone would pick me up soon and I sat and waited on the porch and hoped it might be Scott who showed up.

It wasn't Scott who picked me up, but his uncle, a handsome man (about my age!) who clearly displayed the genetic roots of Scott's attractiveness. "You're Scottie's friend," he said when he lifted my bag of books and heaved them into the back of the truck. "He said he had a good time out of the lake with you. Shame about your leg. Hope it's feeling better."

I nodded and smiled and we talked about the local landmarks as he drove me back toward the village and the train station. And that was that, my one and only visit to Evan's cabin. Back in the city, it all seemed like it had happened to someone else, as if it were a scene from a movie or out of one of the books I had read.

Months later, however, when Evan was meeting his lover and some other friends at the cabin—he had been unable to leave the city at the same time as the rest of the group—Evan called the car service I had talked about to take him out to the cabin. He described the pickup truck exactly as I had—red and old and clunky and noisy—and mentioned that his driver was an "impossibly handsome young man." It wasn't Scott but his older brother, Ray, who was the driver, and after listening to Ray's litany of the town's landmarks—the Laundromat, the green barn, the new stone bridge—Evan asked Ray about his younger brother, explaining he had heard of Scott from a friend who had used the cabin while his leg was healing.

"He's done flown the coop," Ray said, smiling and laughing as he turned onto the path which led to the cabin. "He got his sorry ass out of here as quick as he wised up to that girl who was chasing him. He never really wanted to stay, you know? He's got the family wild streak bad. He's working down in Florida now, taking tourists out on fishing boats or out sailing. He's out doin' the world. Seein' what he can see."

"I'm glad he went for the adventure," I told Evan when he relayed the story to me later, sometime after my leg had healed and I was once again hunting for a new boyfriend. "Sounds like he's happy—doing what he should be doing."

Half of Hamlet

Some things I never remember: Like don't ask an actor about their show. I made that mistake when I asked Libby how rehearsals were going for *Hamlet*. Libby and I have been working at a midtown media company for more than twenty years. We both started with the company long after we were in our twenties, which means in present time we are in our mid-fifties as well as being outcasts from the professional theater. We spend our days toiling away at thankless corporate jobs, filing legal certificates, opening and closing bank accounts, and changing signatories, waiting for our real lives to begin after hours and on weekends. I left the theater when my ex-boyfriend became a director and refused to cast me in his production, so I became a writer, and in my spare time I wrote a lot of short stories and a couple of novels about boyfriends with bad alibis, dates who never progressed to becoming boyfriends, and a slew of thieves posing as nameless tricks, so I consider myself about as successful at being a writer as I was as acting as an actor, which means a few of my ex-boyfriends bought my books hoping to earn some extra cash by blackmailing me, though I feel certain that they never bothered to read a single word of them or if they did, they quickly realized that if they took me to court, a lot more of their dirt would become public record than was already accessible in a fictional version. Libby went from dreaming of being a Broadway star to dreaming of breaking in a chorus line to dreaming of doing her own cabaret show and then settled with a company of actors who put on productions with puppets. Not puppet shows for kids, but serious-minded attempts at distilling great works of stagecraft to an off-off-off-Broadway audience of friends and co-workers trapped in an airless black box hoping for an intermission that will never arrive. Now in her twelfth season with puppets, Libby has performed in adaptations of *Faust, Tales of Hoffman, Anthony and Cleopatra*, and *Macbeth*.

I should mention that these great works of the legitimate stage presented as annotated puppet dramas are also performed with music and lyrics and singing and choreography, which makes them closer to musical comedy than dramatic opera when you factor in the added impact of an actor singing in a strange puppet voice and dancing like a pogo stick. The music and lyrics are written by the director who also distills these great feats of literature into their puppet adaptations. By professional theatrical standards, the puppet productions are poorly-attended heavily-endowed financial flops, but the theater troupe behind them has parlayed their token notices into international tours and triumphs. Every year Libby has traded in her corporate-earned vacation days to perform in such cities as Tokyo, Sydney, Barcelona, and Paris.

The founder and force behind all of this is a refugee from the once Soviet occupied Ukraine. Yuri is a short, squat man with a shock of white hair that resembles the top of a cotton swab, the sort of guy you would expect to find behind a barber chair and not playing with oversized wooden toothpicks. Yuri found the puppets, or marionettes as they are more accurately named, in a trunk stored in the basement of the ethnic community center in a former church on the Lower East Side, close to the restaurant where I used to go for fried pierogis and sour cream with an ex-boyfriend before he became my ex. There was no clue as to who had left the puppets in the basement or to whom they belonged, so Yuri refurbished the carved figures, designed and sewed new costumes for each of them, and convinced the community center to turn over their ground floor space to his new theater company. According to Libby, Yuri's newest dream is to take his production of *Hamlet* on an Eastern European tour, intent on discovering the workshop where his puppets might have been created.

When I make my mistake and stop Libby in the office hallway and inquire about her rehearsals, she takes a dramatic gasp of air and says, "Oh, Hamlet is depressed."

I try to suppress both a smile and a laugh. "Isn't that the point of the play?" I answer. "That Hamlet is depressed?"

She gives me an expression that says she is in no mood for irony. "The *actor* playing Hamlet is depressed," she says seriously, like any self-focused/self-involved actor who has spent thousands of dollars on diction lessons would.

Of course, the actor is depressed, I think. If he is any good at all. It's called method acting, but maybe in the puppet world it's harder to imbue a piece of wood with emotions and therein lies the rub.

"He's only able to use one arm," Libby adds and I realize that not only does Hamlet have to play Hamlet, albeit an abbreviated version with singing and dancing, but must do so holding a puppet who is also pretending to be Hamlet. I think that would make any seriously trained actor depressed.

"I've been trying to help by holding his puppet but I can't do Ophelia, Gertrude, and half of Hamlet. *And* Rosencrantz and Guildenstern. It's just not possible to stretch me like that. And no one in the audience will believe it. I have been trying to get Yuri to add someone to the cast to help Hamlet hold his puppet, but he is being stubborn and says we're only doing it for one benefit performance and it will ruin his vision. But I've been having to do half of Hamlet's scenes as well as my own. It's exhausting and infuriating and senseless and Yuri is losing his grip. If Hamlet keeps this up, we might just have to cancel the show and if we cancel the show then there is no money raised for a tour! He has us trapped into this."

Libby and I live in a city of unemployed actors. Actors posing as taxi drivers, bartenders, waiters, and vice-presidents of billion-dollar empires. You can't turn a corner without bumping into an actor. "There must be someone who can help," I say, trying to offer some honest sympathy to her plight.

"We've been through three Hamlets already. And Yuri likes Jared."

"Jared?"

"The young man playing Hamlet."

"What about Sean?" I ask Libby. Sean is Libby's husband, an Irish poet-playwright-actor who is also a sometime member of the puppet drama troupe.

"There's so much bad blood there right now," Libby says. "Sean was originally cast as Hamlet but then he wanted to rewrite everything, so we're lucky that Yuri is willing to let him be Claudius and the ghost of Hamlet's father."

"If I were younger and knew the text I'd offer to help," I say, trying once more to appear empathetic.

"Oh, you don't need to know the text," she answers. "Just learn the cues."

She stares at me, waiting for me to back away. When I don't, she says, "Let me call Yuri. I'm sure we can use you. It's only for one night."

* * *

Back at my desk I fret over what has just transpired. Did I just volunteer to play with a puppet over the weekend or was I trapped and coerced into it by a wickedly deceitful self-involved actor pretending to be a co-worker and friend? For a moment I imagine what it would be like to be on stage, holding a puppet in a spotlight, performing Shakespeare, reciting Hamlet's soliloquies, basking in the glory of applause. I have visions of handing a resignation letter to my manger, of first-class flights and luxury hotel rooms, and fans waiting for autographs at the stage door. I no longer have a working acting resume and try to imagine my response when the director asks me what skills I have to play half of Hamlet. I mentally compile a list of Hamlet-type roles I have performed in my all-too short stage career as a male ingenue. Prince Dauntless in *Once Upon a Mattress*. Hero in *A Funny Thing Happened on the Way to the Forum*. Charlie Brown in *You're a Good Man, Charlie Brown*. And I'm convinced that because they are all musical comedies my prior acting credits will also show that I am already adept at singing and dancing.

A few minutes later Libby pops her head into my cubicle and says all is well, not to worry, "Yuri has found someone to play half of Hamlet."

I smile and nod and return to work on the legal report I am preparing to file with a state agency, relieved that I don't have to convince myself to return to the stage and imagine, instead, returning to my apartment and an ice-cold glass of wine and a weekend of no stress. At the end of the day, as I am putting on my coat, Libby reappears. "Oh, good," she says, "You're still here. We need you after all."

Before I can even ask for an explanation, she offers one up. "Yuri had an argument with the actor he wanted, so now we need another actor."

I neither agree nor disagree to accept the role, thinking I might as well do this until I am told I am no good at it and then offer to be a bartender at the benefit, just to appease Libby because we have been friends since the dark ages of our youth and you never know when you will need to collect on brownie points, so I follow her out into the hallway, down the elevator, and into the subway. As we cross midtown, she gives me puppet lessons, or puppet pointers. "Don't try to bob the puppet head when you are speaking as a puppet, but make sure the puppet's eyes face the audience, not another puppet, but you can twist the rod to turn the head to show a facial reaction." I know from having seen several of her productions that the actors holding the handles and strings are as visible as the puppets, but I forgot how hideous the puppets look until we arrive at the performance space at the community center on the Lower East Side where the one-night benefit of *Hamlet* will be performed. The puppets are approximately two feet tall with exaggerated noses and mouths and eyes that make them look more comical than dramatic. A steel rod rises out of the center of the skull—or wig or hat, depending on the puppet—and there are strings attached to the arms and feet. Each puppet is dressed in a brightly colored costume with frills at the neck and sleeves, the sort of which a circus clown might wear.

Libby lifts a particularly grotesque-looking puppet and brings it over to me, a bald man with clown-white skin, giant muttonchop sideburns, a handlebar moustache, and a goatee. "O that this too too solid flesh would melt," she says in a low, sing-songy voice, and shows me how to move the puppet wand and strings. Just as I realize that she has been reciting Hamlet's dialogue and that this dreadful-looking marionette just might be Hamlet himself, or, rather, the puppet Hamlet, a short man with white hair skulks onto the stage and stares at us. When Libby notices him, he says directly to her (and not the puppet she is holding), "No, he won't do. He's all wrong."

I realize he is talking about me and I let the puppet handle dangle. "You haven't even given him a chance," she says.

"I don't need someone like him."

I am aware that I have been insulted, but I am not entirely sure what the insult was. I've always tried to be a likeable fellow. I know from years of looking at myself in mirrors and other shiny reflective surfaces that my resting face is a frown so I must smile and lift my eyes to appear more likeable, which I do now as I look between the grotesque puppet and the glowering man that I know for a fact is Yuri.

"He's too much of a distraction!"

I'm still uncertain what the insult is: my weight, my height, my lack of a chin, my haircut? It's true that I lost my hairline in my forties, but what remains has been handsomely streaked with gray and white. In fact, I realize I look rather similar to Yuri, albeit a likeable and optimistic version of him when I am smiling, which is what I am trying to do now.

"You might as well call it off then," Libby says. "You can cancel the benefit and the tour because I am not going to perform half of Hamlet."

I see the tension rise in Yuri's eyes and posture, even though he still disregards me. "Look at him and tell me if you think he is right. You've been with this company for—how long? Tell me—honestly—"

I realize that it is now Libby's turn to insult me and she politely chokes on her thoughts and words. After a dramatic pause she says, "This is the theater. Everyone is welcome. On stage and off. You of all people have no right to criticize."

On the surface I thought it would be fun and easy—singing and dancing with puppets, but I realize I am in over my head on all things relating to dramatic marionettes and I'm ready to call it quits—or be fired—when I see someone standing beside Yuri. He is taller than Yuri—almost anyone is taller than Yuri, but this fellow looks like an Olympic athlete. At first glance you might think that Yuri and this fellow could be father and son, except that they bear no resemblance to one another and this particular "child" is no child at all, but a handsome young man who appears to be in his early twenties, swarthy as a seaman, gorgeous and overly muscled and wearing the sort of singlet that an Olympic wrestler would wear. From a distance I am immediately aware of his wide shoulder span, thick biceps, narrow waist, furry thighs, and a chest full of hair that sprouts skyward like a field of wild grass in the moonlight.

"Most certainly we could use the help," the young man says, striding toward me and shaking my hand. He introduces himself as Jared. His voice is raspy, but his diction is precise and trained. His hand is meaty and the shake is firm. I fall immediately in love with him, then realize that he could never be as faithful and devoted to me as I would be to him so I mentally break up with him before he breaks my heart. All this happens in a millisecond, shorter than our clasp of hands. It's a survival instinct I have honed from years of being smitten and rejected by unattainable, overly attractive men.

Jared takes the hideous puppet from me and I catch a smell of the woodsy-musky fragrance of his skin and hair and muscles when he turns and stands in front of me so that my eyes are level with the center spot of his back. I am mortified because I realize I must pull in my stomach so that it doesn't press against his lower back and the top curve of his ass and, as I make this uncomfortable physical adjustment, I realize my groin is swelling with desire. Jared instructs me to wrap my arms around his body so that I can manipulate the rod and strings of the puppet he is holding. "See," he says to Yuri. "A natural fit."

I peer around a meaty shoulder blade and see Yuri and his anger. Or envy. Who wouldn't want to put his arms around this young muscle stud? I think of all the names he might be called on social media posts: muscleboi, sex-in-a-singlet, eyecandy, alphatoy. I am dizzy with fear and desire and smiley emoticons.

Jared shifts and tilts his eyes down to mine. "Can you sing?" he asks, as if we were on a date.

I am lost in the rich blackness of his eyes as I answer, "I love to sing."

Jared shifts again and says to Yuri, "If he wears white, he could also be the ghost of Hamlet's father."

I see Libby lift her eyes in fear of this suggestion. "Yuri, we agreed that Sean would play the ghost," she says.

"It doesn't make any sense for him to be the ghost if he is already playing Claudius," Yuri responds.

"But you have me playing Ophelia and Gertrude!" Libby wails back.

"It might solve the Rosencrantz problem," Jared says.

"Yuri, may I have a word?" a man's voice sounds from the back of the room.

I look out into the empty seats of the audience and see Sean, Libby's husband, talking with another man, who also seems familiar to me, but I can't quite place how I know him. Defeat and resignation overcome Yuri. He slumps his shoulders and mutters something that I am certain is an expletive and walks off stage toward Sean. Libby strides off behind Yuri and Jared and I are left alone.

"I didn't mean to cause all this trouble," I say to Jared and repeat the sentiment to Sean when everyone but the familiar-looking man return to the stage area and I am informed that my role has been expanded to be the ghost of Hamlet's father.

The next hour is spent explaining blocking and cues and how to hold a puppet. I follow Yuri and Jared around the stage, learning the role of the ghost of Hamlet's father and inhaling the masculine fragrance of the alphatoy-muscleboi prince. Libby stops a scene because of acid-reflux. Sean speaks in English accent that sounds like jabberwocky. Yuri takes the opportunity to display his machismo with his booming baritone and vise-like grips and shoves, and I can tell he particularly likes to man-handle Jared, clutching him at the waist or shoulders as if he were trying to tame a stallion. I try to make mental notes on cues and lines, but all I can focus on is Jared and his muscles and wonder why he is able to only lift one arm—though I can't tell which arm he can't lift because he seems to use both without any visible disability. At one point I get lost in the swarthy stubble of his face, recalling the way my lips would burn and chap after spending an evening kissing an ex-boyfriend who had a heavy facial scruff.

My arms tire as I keep the puppet handle suspended and when I occasionally dip my arm to relieve the stress, Yuri bellows, "You must keep the arms up!" I can't remember the last time I went to the gym—I abandoned my membership when I saw two ex-boyfriends having sex together in the steam room, but even at my most physical prime I doubt I could keep these puppets suspended without a break. No wonder Jared is depressed; I'm certain he doesn't want to perform with a puppet. I'm certain that the weight of his magnificent plump biceps must make them extra-hard to keep them suspended alongside a steel puppet rod. It is only when we are rehearsing my presence in the "get-thee-to-a-nunnery" scene between Hamlet and Ophelia that Hamlet loses an arm. His left arm to be precise. The arm falls out of the socket of the puppet torso and suddenly there is a tangle of strings. Yuri booms out a string of expletives and then adds, "I thought I had fixed that!"

On stage, Yuri says sternly to me, as if I am the cause of all this mess, "This is where you can be of the most help." He proceeds to show me how to turn a ghost father into an emergency puppet medic by twisting the wooden arm back into the socket of the torso of the puppet.

We continue the scene and the arm falls out again. While the action continues, I swirl around Jared and Libby attempting to reclaim the puppet arm. As I catch it and struggle to reinsert it into the puppet's torso while the live-action actors do a dance routine, I am suddenly aware that I have either been misinformed or I have misinterpreted the situation. The human Hamlet might be depressed, but there is nothing wrong with his arm or arms. In fact, the human Hamlet has gorgeous arms. It is the hideous puppet portraying Hamlet that has only one working arm. Performing "half of Hamlet" means keeping the left arm of a puppet in place and this could make any actor frustrated—and depressed. But a solution to all of this seems so obvious to me: Why don't they just use another puppet? Why doesn't someone just go to a toy store and buy a Pinocchio puppet and put a paper crown on him? And the truth is: No one in the audience is even going to look at a puppet Hamlet when the live-action version is a handsome muscleboi alphatoy sent down from Mount Olympus!

When Jared, Libby, and Sean take breaks and the familiar looking man who has been sitting in the audience gathers them into another group conversation, I learn a song that belongs to the character of the ghost of Hamlet's father. Yuri glowers at me, changing every vowel to syllables. The young man at the keyboard is named Garret, with thin arms and bony fingers that I think will break if he plays the keys too loud, the tones filtered through a speaker system to sound like a carousel tune. I am grateful that the song is tuneless Sprechstimme and I do not need to carry a puppet to portray a ghost. The plan that is unfolding is that I will wear a white or gray tunic, and at the benefit performance tomorrow night I will be able to perform the song with the written lyrics and score on a music stand. I now feel like everyone is accepting me as part of their little puppet troupe. "Don't worry about the melody," Garret whispers to me when Yuri is distracted by Sean animatedly talking to the familiar-looking man in the audience. "Just learn the rhythm."

Our rehearsing is interrupted when the familiar-looking man approaches the piano. Seeing him closer and in the full light of the stage, I am suddenly aware I know him. My mood instantly changes to the worse. We are ex-boyfriends from a galaxy far, far away. And he hasn't changed a bit—well, perhaps maybe more gray hair and a slimmer, more distinguished and professional composure, whereas I haven't aged so gracefully and am immediately aware of that fact. "Bryce," I say when our eyes meet. "How did you find your way here?"

"I became one of the trustees about two years ago," he says. "And you?"

I explain my office friendship with Libby, and Bryce and I do polite, quick catch-ups—where we are living, who we know in common who is still working in the theater. Our breakup was contentious. It inspired a painfully bitter short story that was published in a notable anthology and won an important but cashless literary award.

"There's a lot of unfinished business we need to work out," he says as the others are returning to the stage.

"Not really," I answer, feeling my chest wheezing from the unexpected anxiety. I have no desire to get to know Bryce again or relive the misery of those days with or without him. "There's nothing to repair between us."

My tone is unfriendly. I notice the astonished expressions of confusion and disbelief on my fellow actors' faces that could never be replicated by a puppet. And in a flash, it all makes sense to me, though I have no confirmation of my suspicions. Bryce is from old money, old Connecticut banking-insurance money, and he was always attracted to overly muscled guys, guys who reminded him of his first love, Joey, who ended up becoming my boyfriend when he moved to Manhattan. I suspect that Yuri is "happy" with Jared because Bryce and his money are "happy" with Jared and which may be the root of the conflict with Sean—and Libby, who are not happy because Sean's talent is being pushed to the side for a young muscleboi with big arms, a clone of Joey if there ever was one.

As Bryce strides away, Libby pulls me aside. "What did Bryce say?" she asks. "It's the first time we are doing a show without Yuri as a performer. If we can do this, Sean and I can convince the rest of the trustees that the troupe has longevity in case Yuri doesn't want to continue with the theater."

I see her concern. I see the sweat around her eyes. I see her make up caking in the folds of the character lines at the sides of her mouth. But I am frozen in place, unable to continue. "It's a bit more complicated," I say.

I haven't seen Bryce in more than twenty years and I feel my body quickly shutting down on me. My steps are wooden. I can't lift my arms. I can't focus. Depression overwhelms me. All I want to do is quit, walk out of the theater, and never lift the strings of another puppet. I don't want to be anywhere near Bryce. Bryce strides onto the stage again and whispers in my ear, "Let's have a little talk." The others scatter and Bryce leads me into a dark area in the audience where I can barely focus on his face.

"Whatever you're feeling about me, don't let it hurt the others or the performance," he says. "I stood up for you when Yuri wanted you out."

My anger flares. "I volunteered," I respond. "So, stop pretending you are doing me a favor. I don't owe you anything."

"I'm not the villain here," he says.

"But you are," I answer. "You walked out on Joey."

"That was a long time ago. And you know I had to do it. I couldn't turn down that job. I'm sorry and I wish I could tell Joey I'm sorry. Don't you think I relive that mistake over and over? But it's been years. *Years.* And I want this benefit to go on as much as the others do."

I am ready to give it all up and walk away when he says the magic words, the phrase that will make me stay. "No one's going to try and stop you from telling this story. Write whatever you need to write for us to get to the end of this."

"This?" I ask, knowing the meaning is more than a one-night benefit performance.

"This," he answers.

* * *

Bryce was always headed to New York. He saw his first stage musical at the age of eight, an out-of-town tryout in New Haven. He was stage-struck, quick-witted, and driven to succeed. The theater ignited a passion in him—trips to record stores to buy cast albums, trips to music stores to find scores, plans to share his new-found expertise and overtake his high school drama club.

Joey was a muse. An investment. A puppet Bryce could control, at least for a while. A good-looking boy with a sweetness you wanted to know and possess. Joey didn't understand plot points and structures and act breaks but he would practice choreography and dance steps to perfection like an athlete. Bryce cast Joey as Sky Masterson in their high

HALF OF HAMLET

school production of *Guys and Dolls* and their lives were changed forever. They were inseparable until Bryce's passion outgrew Joey and Joey's focus expanded. Sex was never an obstacle for either of them, but it was what kept them together and pulled them apart.

Bryce moved to the West Village after college. I met him when we both worked for a theater company in Chelsea. Bryce was already the assistant company manager. I took a job trying to do group sales and hoping it might provide me with a foot-in-the-door opportunity for an acting role. One day I was the new kid in the office and Bryce had to know everything about me. The next, I was just another person he had bedded and gossiped about until I told him that it was miserable way to live.

I was poor and struggling and looking for new friends and an opening into the professional theater. I gave up a tiny studio I couldn't afford so I could find another one I could share. That was when Joey came into town. Joey had stayed behind in Connecticut, accepting a job with an insurance company and pretending to date women to appease his family. Bryce told him about the apartment to share and Joey moved in with me. We lived together until Bryce decided that he wanted Joey back.

Bryce and Joey shared an early, young history together that no one else could erase. I was a part of it but also apart from it. There was always more than one story and one side to any story. There was Bryce leaving Joey, Joey leaving me, Joey loving Bryce more, Bryce leaving Joey again. Interpretations vary with time and distance and memory and politics, just like a Shakespearian drama. But the ending never changes for me. Joey tested HIV-positive. Bryce left to take a job in California and did not return to help and support Joey. Joey never came out to his family and I became his family. I went with him to doctors and clinics and rallies and demonstrations. We marched and protested until he could not do it anymore. I knew that Bryce and I were mismatched just as Joey and I

112

were, but I fought for Joey. The last few months of his life he moved in with me again, sharing the apartment in the West Village he had once abandoned. In the end I surrendered him to the family who had turned their back on him because I could not afford to pay for his funeral. Bryce and Joey's families had been friendly for generations. Bryce flew back from California to attend the funeral in Connecticut and, because I was an outsider, I was not invited to attend.

* * *

The next morning when I get out of bed my feet are swollen; my shoulders and back ache. I want to amputate all of my limbs and only be a floating brain in a glass jar. My thighs have become bricks. Even my fingernails hurt. Lying in bed I practice the breathing techniques I learned when I slept with an ex-boyfriend who was a computer repair technician who taught yoga on the side. I shift and slide my way out of bed to make coffee.

I take painkillers. I try to relax, but with every movement I writhe with pain. I don't think any story is worth this much pain. I spent several sleepless hours arguing in my mind with Bryce, then arguing with myself, then remembering Joey and missing him. I know the years since have reshaped my memories of him. I have forgotten the bad times, focused on the good ones; some of the truth lost somewhere and a lot of memories and details lost. I decide to abort my plan to be half of Hamlet. Once my head clears, I will call Libby and tell her my decision.

I fall asleep for about an hour but when I wake the pain is still there, though duller. I check my skin for shingles and insect bites and any probable allergic rashes and spend an hour checking symptoms on the internet. I avoid phoning Libby. I have more mental fights with Bryce and even more with myself. I decide I won't run away from a problem like Bryce did. I won't be indecisive like Hamlet. I won't be unsupportive of Libby. I take a hot shower and more painkillers and that seems to help. I dress and gingerly make my way to the subway and across town to the live-action puppet theater.

When I walk into the large area that is used as a dressing room, Hamlet is seated on the floor with his legs extended. He is shirtless and only wearing briefs. "Oh good," he says when he sees me. "I'm glad you got here early. You can help me stretch." My groin swells with such desire that I temporarily forget about my own pain and mental struggles.

I hold his ankles as he lies on his back and stretches his arms above his head. He arches his back so that his stomach muscles show their muscles. I can see the outline of the head of his penis. It is like a giant mushroom in a forest of black hair. He slowly rises into a sit up and wraps his hands around mine at his ankles.

He asks me if I will knead his shoulders. I realize my mouth is open in astonishment and I do a slight brush of my fingers over my lips to make sure I am not drooling, but I agree to help him, thinking that becoming closer to Jared might be a way of stirring up Bryce's jealousy.

Hamlet rolls over on his stomach and tells me to straddle him. I might have blushed if all of my blood was not already at my groin. In this position I can see the full parting of his ass cheeks because of the strain of the sheer fabric of his briefs. I look around for hidden security cameras or police officers. Surely this is a ploy. Somehow this is Bryce's revenge on me for something I didn't realize I had ever done. Entrapment is only seconds away or this will replay over the internet and reach three hundred million views without ever paying me a dime.

I knead Hamlet's skin and muscles and hair. How can I not do this? At my age and weight class and lack of self-esteem?

His flesh reddens. He sweats. The space is filled with his woodsy-musky fragrance. I think I could reach ejaculation without anyone even touching me.

"That's terrific," he says. When he rolls over my eyes drop to his protrusion. His briefs are wet. "Do you want me to do you?"

He says it as if he had just had an orgasm and it is now my turn.

I want it so badly I think I could cry. "I'm too sore," I say, which is the truth.

"Sore? Like how?"

My response is a weak, "Everywhere."

He tells me to sit on the stool in front of the make-up mirror. He says he has an ointment that works wonders. "I'll do you and then you can do me."

His next request is absolutely horrifying. "Take off your shirt."

I know there are genres of gay fetishes. Even subgenres of subgenres. Leathermen wearing vinyl masks. Hairless bears. Sumo wrestlers wearing diapers. But to my knowledge there is no one gay or straight who lusts after an aging troll. In front of the mirror I see my hair exploding at the sides of my ears like a clown. But I am a clown without the cartoon makeup so I am nothing but a hideous aging troll. No one fetishizes an aging troll. I can't look away from my reflection without thinking, *How did this ever happen to me? I've become a hideous looking puppet!*

Love is blind, or that is how I interpret Hamlet's methodical and doctorly application of an ointment to my shoulders, arms, and back. The scent is musky and woodsy, just as he is. I begin to feel a light tingling that eases the aches, as if hummingbirds are beating beneath my skin.

Grateful as a geisha, I slip my T-shirt back on and rub the ointment on Hamlet's body, mimicking his professionalism as if I were an apprentice masseuse.

It's another bonding moment, but I want to know more of Hamlet, or, rather, of Jared. I only have a sixth sense that he is having an affair with Bryce or that there is some unexplained connection between them. But even more, I want to know if he could ever find true happiness with a troll. An aging gay troll who only wants to be adored like a clown in a circus but will settle for being man-handled like a hideous-looking puppet. Then I realize I don't even know if Jared is gay.

"What's your theory about Hamlet?" I ask him.

"What do you mean?" he responds. I feel the darkness of his voice move through his bones and muscles and skin and hair.

"Why Hamlet's depressed."

"Isn't it obvious? His uncle murdered his father and his mother was part of the crime."

"That's why it's probably not true. Shakespeare was way too clever to be obvious."

"Then what's your theory?"

"Well, I think everyone is gay, or has a range of gayness," I say, the way an ex-boyfriend once explained it to me, continuing to rub the ointment into Jared's skin and muscles. He doesn't tense at the mention of the words "gay" or "gayness," which might mean he doesn't object to it, but it's his defense of character I am more interested in. "I don't think he's struggling with his homosexuality," I add. "He's struggling with his acceptance of it."

Jared tenses. "Some people see being gay as a disability," he says.

"Like Hollywood and casting directors," I add.

"Family, too," he says. "His father might see him as less than a man because he was gay."

There it is. Or at least it is the basis of my new theory: Jared is not out to his family. Hence, his depression, or at least a large chunk of it. And he probably doesn't want to bring home to his family a creepy, rich boyfriend like Bryce who is probably older than his dad. But Jared's next response is unexpected because it means he has given some thought to this idea before I ever raised the issue of it.

"Your theory is wrong," Jared says. "When Shakespeare wrote Hamlet there was no sense of someone having a gay identity because the concept didn't exist."

"That's correct on a historical level," I answer. "But not an emotional one."

"You might be right on that," he says. "There was probably gaydar before there was a name for it. My mom knew about me before I did. She had a brother who was gay."

"Are you still close with her?"

"She's always texting me! She hates that I am in this show. She thinks I am messing up my life. She wants me to get a job with a decent paycheck."

Ah, there's the rub. The truth behind the truth. Hamlet is depressed because his mother doesn't want him to work in the theater.

As I wipe the ointment off my hands and Hamlet slips into his singlet, my fellow puppeteers arrive and change into their costumes. Libby reminds me of cues and not to chase the puppet Hamlet's arm during the get-thee-to-a-nunnery scene. "Just let it flop around. When the scene is over, we'll snap it back in."

The next hour we walk through the script. The room is now full of tables. The catering staff ignores us and sets out plates and silverware and trays for the buffet tables. Waiters dressed in tuxedos begin placing glasses on the tables. I expect to see Bryce at any moment, striding toward me to start a new argument, but he remains purposely absent.

Suddenly, I feel nervous and hot, as if my skin is afire. I lift my tunic to make sure I am not developing a rash from the ointment or that the hummingbirds are not using their beaks to break through the surface of my skin. Then, I am suddenly tired. I find a chair in the back room and sit and close my eyes and practice my slow, yoga breathing. I fall asleep until I am roused sometime later by Libby. "There you are," she says. "We're going on in ten minutes."

As I wake and walk, I realize my body still aches and my head feels heavy. I remember I haven't eaten anything at all today and I am suddenly fearful of a headache growing worse while on stage because I am hungry.

To the side of the dressing area are trays of cookies and pastries for the after-performance mingling. Just as I take a bite from what looks like a brownie, I see Jared approaching me.

"You're going to regret eating that," he says.

"Why?"

"Those are Yuri's brownies. He laces them."

"What do you mean?"

Bryce laughs. "You'll see soon," he says. "Be sure to drink some water."

I finish the brownie and reach for a bottle of water from the buffet table. Bryce follows behind me as if he wants to tell me something important.

"Sara wants to know if you'll have drinks with her after the show."

"Sara?

"Yes, Joey's sister."

"Why is Sara coming to the performance?"

"I thought you knew."

"Knew what?"

"Jared is Sara's son," he says. "Joey's nephew. My godson."

I stare at him to make sure he is telling me the truth. "Does Jared know about me?" I ask. "About me and Joey?"

"Of course not," Bryce answers. "You refused to be part of his family."

* * *

And then it begins. I am onstage and everything is a blur. It's as if my genetic makeup has been rearranged from the ointment and the spiked brownie and the unsettling information and memories. I interrupt dialogue to point out for the audience the hideous and unflattering characteristics of the puppets, noting that the puppet Ophelia is a foot taller than all the other puppets and she creates an imbalance to the plot and I beg the audience to overlook this fault. I point out the disparities of the accents the actors use, mock the baby voices Sean creates for the castle guards, and I invent a dance step while Hamlet sings "what a piece of work is man." I provide commentary on the backstory of Hamlet and Ophelia, questioning their loyalty and sexuality, not to mention their difference in heights and ages. I wander from scene to scene, trying to shake thoughts back into my mind. The audience is a small gathering of friends and loyal sponsors of the theater company, less than a hundred guests scattered around ten tables. I wander off stage and eat from bread baskets because I am famished and ask the audience directly, "Why, oh why, do we need a puppet version of *Hamlet*?" My cast mates sweep me from scene to scene, not daring to pin me to a chair because I might impact their own performance. The performing area under the lights is intensely hot. I watch Hamlet drip with sweat. I tell the audience how wonderful it is to watch Hamlet sweat, that Shakespeare got it all wrong because watching Hamlet sweat is beauty, not torture. I sing my song with new lyrics I make up on the spot. At one point I ask Jared what drug was in the ointment he used to soothe my pain, changing the entire context of the play as if Hamlet had murdered his father. Jared gives me a glassy-eyed fearful stare, the same as Libby and Sean. Sean escorts me off stage and whispers some harsh jabberwocky in my ear, but somehow, I return. The audience response is a mixture of laughter and disbelief and, when all the dead bodies are on stage, I give an impromptu speech on the power of laughter to heal depression because Hamlet's inability to act has set us all free from our miserable captivity in the theater.

Hours later I wake in my apartment, my mouth dry and sore. I have no memory of how I found my way back home after the show, though I recall wind rushing through the open window of a taxi.

* * *

Back at my desk the following day, starting another work week, I avoid walking by Libby's cubicle. Later in the morning, she appears by my desk. "You were lucky," she says.

"I didn't know about the brownie," I tell her. "So, I didn't know how it was going to affect me. I haven't had pot in more than twenty years. Since Joey lived with me."

"He was such a nice man," she says.

For a moment I am confused and she catches my forgetfulness.

"Remember?" she says. "Long before we started here. Before I met Yuri. Joey was the assistant stage manager on that awful production of the Sam Shepard workshop I was in."

"I completely forgot. Wasn't Bryce the assistant producer?"

"No, that was a later show. I was his sister's roommate in college. Don't you remember? Sara. Joey's sister. And she told me to help her brother get the job."

I nod and then it all comes flooding back. I had forgotten those details. About Sara. And Libby. How distraught they were in the final weeks of Joey's illness when he finally told a few of his family and friends that he was dying and all they wanted to do was help and he didn't want any of them around. Bryce's shame was leaving Joey. Mine was walking away from Joey's family when they wanted to know the whys and what was happening.

"You've kept in touch with her?"

"We're close again thanks to the internet," she answers.

"Why didn't you tell me Bryce was one of the producers?"

"It didn't occur to me," she says. "And then when it did it was too late; you were already talking to him."

"Did he ask Jared to be in the show?"

120

"Sara pushed Bryce for it when she heard of the search for a new Hamlet. She thought it might get acting out of his system."

"Did it?"

"Of course not. And she thought you were very entertaining."

"Was I that bad?"

"Beauty is in the eye of the beholder," Libby answers. "And there's no such thing as a bad actor."

We see one of our managers approaching my workspace and know we have to cut our conversation short. Before she leaves my desk, she hands me a sheet of paper. "You might want to read this."

It is a review of the benefit performance by a well-known theater critic.

"Something magical happened in Denmark at the recent benefit performance of *Hamlet* by the Yuri Kozub Marionette Theater Company. The ghost of Hamlet's father appeared on stage in the form of an uncredited actor and interpreted the stench that was present in Denmark and elsewhere. Shakespeare's most celebrated drama was transformed into a commedia dell'arte masterpiece as the ghost—and the actor portraying the ghost—shepherded Hamlet and a troupe of "hideous and grotesque marionettes" through a wicked and witty satire of the purgatory and pleasures of live theater, moving the ghost center stage as the "unfortunate fool of life and love" who dares members of the audience to escape the "limbo of Hamlet's libido" and risk boredom in their own lives if they do not "ironically witness" his son's inability to make a decision. Yuri Kozub, who directed but did not perform in this lively adaptation of actors, marionettes, and music, should be commended for allowing an actor—and his audience—the creativity to redefine a masterpiece. The ghost's closing speech at the conclusion of the play was a tour de force of the artistic imagination. The theater company is planning an international tour of *Hamlet* later this year."

* * *

Yuri did not ask me to join the company's Eastern European tour though he used my presence in the review to raise money from various cultural organizations and government sponsors and fund his revised production of *Hamlet*. As a publicity stunt, he flew his "hideous and grotesque marionettes" first class and accommodated them in luxury hotel suites. Libby went on tour but Sean did not. In the aftermath of losing the spotlight and his onstage confidence, Sean filed for divorce and returned to Ireland to open a poet's café. Jared also did not go on the tour; he accepted a role in a production in Los Angeles, and, in another twist of irony, a revival of the same Sam Shepard play his mother had once helped Joey get the production job. Sara and Bryce flew out for the opening night performance, but before Jared left town, I met him for dinner and told him my version of the story of his uncle. I learned he had been told much of the same story by his mother and Bryce, only my role had been played by an unnamed "friend in the city."

On the Eastern European tour, Yuri took over the role of Hamlet's father, and a new Hamlet and Claudius were hired. After reading an article on the marionette theater company's tour, an official with the Ukrainian Ministry of Culture had the marionettes seized as stolen cultural antiquities and the tour was cut short. A few months later the community center in the East Village shuttered and the performance space was sold. The purchaser is Bryce. We continue to be friends and not friends; he remains a part of my life but also apart from it. He has asked me to join his new theater company and I've told him yes, on the condition that I can write whatever story I want to tell and from whatever point of view I have of it.

Performing it, however, remains optional.

My Night with Rudolph Valentino

Years ago, after a business trip to San Francisco, I decided to drive to Los Angeles to see a college friend. I rented a car and took the scenic route south, driving along State Route 1, a highway which rims the Pacific coast. It was a long and thrilling day trip, driving around the scenic mountain curves, ragged rocks, and through stretches of redwood forests. By the time I reached Hearst Castle and finished a tour in the late afternoon, I knew I would not complete the journey to Los Angeles that day, and was recommended a hotel further south in Santa Maria.

It was an old, historic inn located inland on the hot, dry stretch of a valley at the base of the Sierra Madres. The interior of the hotel lobby and meeting areas were decorated as if it were a pub in the English countryside, with dark wood paneling, somber rugs, oversized chairs, stained glass windows, and brass chandeliers. The management of the hotel had decided to play up its celebrity prestige—guests used to stop here en route to Hearst Castle from Los Angeles—and silent film movie-star memorabilia decorated the walls and the guest rooms were named after many who had stayed at the hotel: Charlie Chaplin, Marlene Dietrich, Jean Harlow, and Douglas Fairbanks.

My room on the second floor, however, had been named after a local politician, with a window that opened out onto an interior courtyard that was shared by several rooms. As I drew the curtains closed, I noticed that the window was unlocked, and I bolted and tested it to make sure it was secure.

After a long shower and a change of clothes, I was hungry and headed downstairs to the hotel's restaurant, but a wedding reception was in progress in one of the banquet rooms, so I settled in at the bar where it was quieter, ordered a drink and something to eat. From where I was seated I could see the other end of the bar and, as the summer daylight stretched its last breath out, the details of one of the customers seated alone near the door became more distinct. He was tall and slender, probably in his late twenties, and he had a sleek, elegant look about him—slicked-back black hair, a light stubble of beard, a strong sloping nose with flaring nostrils, and a prominent chin, and he was wearing a white shirt open at the collar with an unraveled bow tie draped around his neck. Because of his attire, I took him to be part of the wedding party. I shifted and squirmed on my bar stool, hoping he might notice me, but he seemed distracted and vacuous, intent on downing his drink, and I lost sight of him when a gentleman sat beside me at the bar and began to complain about the noise of the piano in the other room.

An hour later I stumbled up to my room, slipped out of my clothes and into a T-shirt and sweatpants. I considered watching television for a while, but I couldn't find the remote control, so I flipped off the light and pulled back the curtains to look out at the courtyard.

It was empty and unused. The moon was high and strong and it gave my room an eerie blue glow and I drew the curtains together so only a small ray of light came into the room.

I was in a deep sleep when the knock at the door woke me. As I groggily got out of bed, I thought it might be the guy from the bar, come knocking for some companionship instead of handing out more complaints.

I flipped on the light and opened the door but no one was there. I was confused, bewildered, and disappointed, the brighter light of the hall exasperating, and I tried to brush the annoying disturbance away as the immature hijinks of one of the wedding guests. But as I moved to close the door I felt something move through me which felt like an ice cold wind. A chill ran up my spine and along my arms.

The door closed and I turned back to the room and flipped off the overhead light. The moonbeam fell across the carpet again. That was when I saw him. The slick, black-haired handsome man I had seen earlier at the bar. He was substantive and real and I could not figure out how he had made it around me and into the room without my noticing him. He stood visible in the ray of moonlight and looked as if he were posing for a photograph, his nostrils slightly aflare. As my eyes moved from the window back to the man he began to dematerialize, as if he were on an episode of *Star Trek* and Scotty was beaming him to another place.

My heart was racing and I sat on the edge of the bed to gather my wits. What would the front desk think of me if I called them and told them I had just seen a ghost? Instead of reporting the incident, I drank a glass of water, checked the window was secure and the courtyard was still empty, then went back to bed.

I spent the remainder of the night restless, tossing, sweating, fighting an erection as if someone had curled around me, locked me into a hold, and was trying to alternately smother or arouse me. There was a digital clock beside the bed that I watched change minute by minute, digit by digit. Sometime in the early morning I drifted off to sleep, because when I woke the sunlight striped the floor as it split between the curtains.

I rolled over and noticed the curtains were moving. The window was unlocked and opened and a breeze was coming into the room. I sat up in bed and looked quickly around the room to see if anything was missing. Nothing seemed disturbed—my wallet was in place, the car keys were where

I left them. But in the center of the floor, exactly where I had seen the apparition the night before and where the ray of sunlight now hit the carpet, was a shiny silver object. I got out of bed and lifted it up. It was a ring. Silver with a flat top and an engraved insignia. The sizing was small—it would only fit on my pinky finger. I didn't immediately associate the ring with the ghostly vision I had seen the night before. At the time I found it, I was more concerned that I might have been robbed while I slept.

I slipped the ring into a small, top pocket of my knapsack I rarely opened, intending to hand it over to the front desk clerk when I checked out. But that good intention slipped by me because I quickly forgot about it.

The ring stayed in the top pocket of my knapsack for years, forgotten, snug in its upper berth, traveling with me to London, Zurich, Tokyo, and other not so far-off destinations. I only discovered it again when my boyfriend Kurt and I were in Fort Lauderdale and I was emptying the knapsack so that I could use it to carry a towel to the beach. Kurt looked at the ring, smirked and said, "What Cracker Jack box did this come from?"

I explained how I came to find the ring. Kurt thought my ghost sighting was hogwash. Kurt was all numbers; he managed a brokerage office and was also something of an elitist snob, but he could accurately assess the financial value of any item and he dismissed the pinky ring as cold, cheap steel. We were in the last throes of our relationship and to annoy him, I slipped the ring on my small finger and wore if for a few days, until we returned to New York and I noticed the metal had made my skin turn a sickly greenish-black. I placed the ring in a small ceramic bowl in the bedroom of my Chelsea apartment where I kept a set of formal cufflinks and shirt studs and only discovered it again one night when I was dressing for a formal-attire Halloween dinner party. I slipped on the pinky ring and during cocktails that evening, I told a small group of men my story of finding it only after witnessing a ghost the night before.

A young man said, "You might be the last person to boast that he slept with Rudolph Valentino."

I laughed and replied that that was highly unlikely, but he reached into his pocket and pulled out his cellphone and took a picture of my hand with the pinky ring. I had never associated my ghost and cheap treasure with a celebrity phantom, but the young man said that Valentino had often been a guest at Hearst castle and my description of the ghost seemed to match the actor's. I found this young man charming and throughout the evening, in the various positions we found ourselves, he asked me in his most delightful bedroom voice about the name of the inn, the room number I had stayed it, what time of year I was visiting, and on and on.

A week or so later, the young man emailed me evidence of Rudolph Valentino wearing the ring in several movie stills and publicity photos. I downloaded the pictures to my computer and saw it was a perfect match to the pinky ring I had in my possession. The engraving was unmistakable. Valentino is wearing the ring in photos with actresses Gloria Swanson and Agnes Ayres, in a portrait with his dog, and beside a camel on the set of *The Son of the Sheik*, his final film. Valentino died at the age of thirty-one, roughly the same age as the ghostly man I had seen. And the legendary actor in the photos looks exactly like the phantom I had seen in the bar and my hotel room. The young man who had helped me discover this was a blogger and he said he wanted to write about my night with the ghost of Valentino. He contacted the owner of the hotel where I had stayed years before and discovered that several other guests had reported seeing a ghost in the room I had stayed in and that Valentino had been a frequent visitor to the inn. The blog post about the gay man who had slept with the ghost of Valentino went viral. I was more famous than I could possibly imagine, though I gratefully remained unnamed in the post.

Flash forward a few more years to when a reality TV producer contacted the blogger about Valentino's ghost and the blogger gave the producer my name as the source of the haunting. When the producer called, I told her there wasn't much to say about the ghost. I saw him, he disappeared. I shivered and sweated through a night with an erection that would not end. I could not even admit if Valentino—or his ghost—was a good kisser.

But the producer pressed on and asked if I would consider loaning the ring to film an episode of the TV show. I told her I no longer had it. And that was true. One morning not long ago I noticed it was gone—it wasn't in the ceramic bowl. I remember looking around to see if anything else was missing from my apartment, but nothing was. Since I had last seen the ring I had had many visitors to my apartment: boyfriends, tricks, dates, even a hustler or two. Now, discovering and wearing the ring seems like a feverish dream I might have made up in my youth, and I wonder if my night with Valentino was something I had cooked up just to get attention. Only I am not that sort of guy. Instead, I imagine another man wearing that ring now—someone handsome, sleek, elegant, then one morning finding the ring cheap and tawdry and tossing it away. Something for the next man to find.

What Would Q Do?

At noon, you are still working at your desk eighteen floors above the southern edge of Times Square. It is warmer in your glass office than it is in your icy apartment six blocks away. Outside your office window, "Snowpocalypse" has begun. Your view of New Jersey across the Hudson River has disappeared, something you are not entirely upset about. Forecasters have predicted thirty-six inches of snow. Your colleagues are abandoning their posts, scurrying out of the building to trains, taxis, and buses before they stop running. You are grateful for their panic. You are fifty-nine years old. Your desk is a pile of problems. Your job is to put out fires. Solve corporate mishaps. Repair international mistakes. All by remote, from the keyboard, mouse, and computer screen on top of your desk. No travelling allowed. No expenses incurred. You are grateful your phone has stopped ringing. You are happy your email inbox is empty of new messages.

You remain in the warmth of your office. You use the quiet to catch up on the tasks you are unable to do when you are busy with visitors and meetings. You finish reading a financial report of an Italian subsidiary, update a document about the company's internal business units, and research a labor issue in Brazil. You are writing an email about an employee issue in the Warsaw office when you hear your name echo down the hallway. It is Kristin, one of the attorneys on the floor, saying, "I'm sure he can help you."

Seconds later she arrives at your office door. She is a slim, sharp-witted woman, mother of two children not yet out of day care. There is a wild, fearful look in her eyes that you gather is from her anxiety over lingering too long in the office to make it safely to her suburban home. She is escorting a gentleman that can only best be described as a live-action version of James Bond. He is introduced to you as Harold Somethingoranother. He is over six feet tall, impeccably dressed in a pale blue-gray suit, hand-tailored to reveal every inch of his toned but not overly muscled physique. His eyes match the color of his suit. His hair is wavy, the color of ocean sand, slicked back from his widow's peak in deep rivulets.

You stand when he walks into your office, something you rarely do when visitors arrive. You shake his hand. It is a tight, professional, no-nonsense grip. His greeting and your name arrive with a British accent. Upper crust. Aristocratic. Over educated. And highly confidential.

Everything becomes a roar and a blur. As he explains his dilemma—he is in from Dubai for a sales conference and has a twelve-million-dollar contract that needs to be legalized—your eyes flicker between Kristin and Harold Somethingoranother. You are a fifty-nine-year-old *gay* man, smitten by a new client with spy-killing movie star looks. Your cheeks are flushed. Your ears are burning. Your breathing is shallow. When you ask to review the contract, your voice sounds prissy and weak.

Kristin's worried expression manifests into hand-waving and gestures. She excuses herself, thinking you can handle everything ahead, sliding your office door closed as she leaves. You are now alone with James Bond in the warm, brightly-lit glass aquarium that is your office. He explains that he only has an electronic version of the contract, and it is on his laptop that he holds in his hands. He says he will email it to you, and he flips open the computer. He asks you for the password for the wireless network in the building, something you don't use because you work too much already for your pay grade and refuse to be tethered non-stop to a mobile device. The person you know who could send you the password has already left the building. You are suddenly worried that you cannot easily solve this overly handsome man's problem and get him on his way, when you think of a solution. You ask him to download the contract from his laptop onto a thumb drive that you quickly find in a desk drawer. He smiles and says, what a nifty idea, as if it is so low-tech and old-fashioned.

You examine his contract on your computer. It is a corporate application for a line of credit that has required him to include personal information. His home address, age, date of birth, marital status. The application is bordered by logos of international organizations and associations as color graphics. The printer at your desk only handles black and white ink cartridges. You advise James Bond that the application looks fine and you will send three copies to the mopier down the hallway, a multi-function machine that will print the document in color.

You excuse yourself and leave your office to retrieve the printed document. As you rush down the hall you are thinking:

1. That you are moving much too quickly to seem either professional or age-appropriate.

2. James Bond's age on the application was indicated as thirty-three.

3. You are old enough to be his father.

4. His application said he was single.

5. You are not too old to imagine yourself as his lover.

6. You are smiling at the idea of James Bond waiting for you. How long has that been? A handsome man, waiting for your return?

Back in your office you present Secret Agent 007 with the documents for his signature. He signs and you add a variety of embossed seals and ink stamps to make it official. You tuck the final documents into an envelope and hand them over to him. His problem has been solved. He smiles, stands, shakes your hand, thanks you by name, says, "I'm incredibly grateful. You are a lifesaver." And then he is gone.

You sit at your desk for a minute to gather your wits. You remember every moment of the meeting, as if it were a one-night stand that you did not want to end. You go to the door of your office and look down the hallway, hoping to see a parting image of him, but he is gone. You walk down to Kristin's office, wanting to find a witness who could verify that the meeting took place, that it was a real occurrence, not a silly old queen's mirage in a snow storm. Her office is dark, the glass door locked. She has fled the building. You walk back to your office smiling and shaking your head in disbelief. A few minutes later you are involved with solving a problem in the Istanbul office, where it is not snowing.

You work through the storm, occasionally checking news reports. The city is shutting down. Subway and bus service are being suspended. Driving is banned. Flights are being grounded and canceled. A travel ban is in effect. "Rapidly deepening winter storms are very challenging to predict," a weather service reports. The mayor has even put a squash on food delivery. No Chinese takeout tonight. No Pad Thai, burritos, or pizza brought to your door, courtesy of a bike-riding fiend. Corporate emails arrive suggesting all employees consider safety when traveling and to use discretion if attempting to make it to the office the following day. It looks as if tomorrow will never happen. Snowpocalypse is here.

At the end of the day, you slide on your snow boots, a pair of cheap plastic shoes that bind your feet into more misery than a geisha could ever feel. You layer yourself in a black sweater, a black down vest, a black leather jacket, and a black scarf. So much for having a gay chromosome, you think. You have no fashion style. You have no shopping gene. You are the epitome of urban invisible: a fat black circle of differing fabrics. You find your gloves and knit cap and make your way to the elevator.

Outside the office windows it is dark. Evening arrives early. You cannot see the streets below. The snowing continues. On your floor everyone has left. Motion activated lights have powered down, leaving ominous black holes where there are offices and cubicles. The elevator arrives quickly, but you are startled when it stops on a floor, three stories below. The door opens, and a tall man enters. He is not wearing any winter outerwear. He is dressed in a pale blue-gray suit. He looks at you, leaning down to find your eyes. "What luck!" he says. "My lifesaver! My client has bailed on me. The show is canceled. You don't have any plans, do you? Why not join me for a drink?"

You stand there frozen. It is not a cold frozen. It is a frightened frozen. A terrified frozen that is filled with astonishment, awe, disbelief, and glee. Did James Bond just ask you to have drinks with him? Is this a test? Some kind of a hidden camera scam? What would Q do if Bond asked him for a drink? Not the revamped-young-tech-queer geek version who also happens to be a cute actor, but the elder, cranky gadget-maker. The old man with clown-like graying hair who hasn't shaved in days who fumbles and falters every time Bond shows up. Would Q shrug off an offer like this? Or would he be a good sport and socialize with an overly handsome, younger-than-himself, spy-killing movie star?

You don't remember saying yes. You don't remember shaking your head in agreement. You don't remember smiling or giggling like a school girl. Instead, you remember the flush at your cheeks, your ears burning, your voice rising to an octave only canines can hear.

You follow James Bond through the lobby of your office building and outside into the snowstorm. The chill is a bitter ruler, the wind an evil dominating force. You must blink to keep the snow out of your eyes. But James Bond is unfazed. He doesn't tense. He doesn't alter his posture or his stride. He leads the way, suggesting a drink at his hotel, just across the block.

It is nineteen steps through the snow to the hotel. James Bond makes it in eleven. In the hotel lobby, you shake off the snow. There are wet splotches on the shoulders of your jacket and the knees of your pants. When you pull off your cap you are mortified you might have hat hair. You look around for reflective surfaces as you pat the top of your skull, but you find nothing to ease your horror. You look at James Bond. He is now the special, deluxe version in high definition. In the high-tech lighting of the lobby his hair glistens. His skin sparkles. His smile is even, perfect, pearly white.

A maître d' escorts you to a table beside the expansive floor-to-ceiling windows looking down at a Manhattan panorama of dark, swirling evening snow. The hotel décor is urban modern. Sleek leather cushions, marble top tables. James Bond orders a martini, "shaken, not stirred." You order a glass of wine, hoping it registers as a healthy choice and not a girly one.

He mentions that the hotel has been generous, upgrading his room by juggling cancellations and late minute bookings. He says he has a lovely suite, with all the amenities. You keep him talking, asking him questions about his travel: When did he arrive? How long does he plan to be in the city? Where will he travel next?

The drinks arrive, and you offer a toast to "Snowpocalypse."

"Is that what they're calling this?" he asks. "Isn't that glorious. Truly memorable. I love being in New York. I love that office of yours. What a brilliant view!"

On the corporate scale, he is much higher on the ladder of success than you are. The company where you work has thousands of employees. He is a rock star who earns bonuses, options, and commissions. If he worked in New York, that office would be his. You are a corporate requirement who got an office by longevity and downsizing. But you are both necessary to the survival of the company. You are the gadget the spy-killing movie star needs to stay alive. You tell Harold Somethingoranother that on sunny days, sitting at your desk can be a true pain. Too much sunlight. Too much squinting for a view of New Jersey. You tell him you may need to invest in a pair of sunglasses soon.

You are horrified that you are complaining and try to turn it into a joke, worried he might report you to hundreds of higher ups above your pay grade, or worse, that he might have grown up in New Jersey and hold everything against you the way all people from New Jersey do against people who live in Manhattan. You decide to keep your mouth shut, to deflect any further questions away from yourself, asking him more questions about himself. Does he travel often for his job? What is his favorite place to travel? His favorite hotel?

He loves answering your questions, loves talking about himself. You like listening to his voice, looking at his expressions. It is like being on a yacht gliding along the Mediterranean.

When he is at the bottom of his martini, he smiles and asks you, "You'll stay for bite, mate?" He doesn't wait for your answer, knowing, of course, that no one ever turns down James Bond. He flags a waiter, asks for menus, orders another round of drinks.

He takes command when the waiter arrives with the menu, not letting him disappear to another table. He asks about specials, the house favorite, the chef's best, and the waiter's personal opinion. James Bond decides on a prime cut steak, cooked rare. He suggests the salmon for you because it sounds like a special treat. You don't put up any protest. You wonder where he has been all your life. Why can't James Bond order all your meals? Why can't he make all of your decisions?

He talks about the office in Dubai, the high profile of the company in the region. You learn he grew up in London and Cairo, speaks Arabic and French, studied Middle Eastern politics in college, and graduated with honors. You avoid mentioning anything about yourself, fearful that he will lose interest in the tedious humdrum of your life at the center of the most important city of the world. The wine is making you sleepy, the snowing outside is making you dizzy, but the night flies by because you are giddy in love. He has not removed his jacket, not even unbuttoned it or loosened the collar of his shirt or moved his tie, but you have seen his chest expand, rise and fall as he breathes and speaks, his biceps curl and unfurl as he drinks and eats, his lips glide across his teeth as he smiles. His eyes brighten and widen when he describes his passion for surfing in Fiji, his Adam's apple floats up and down his long neck as he sips his martini. You imagine him in a wet suit carrying a surfboard. This is better than TV. Better than a Broadway show. Much better than any Bond movie ever made.

As dinner progresses, you learn he has a younger brother who was married the year before in London to a girl James Bond had once dated. Now the super-secret agent has a current girlfriend in Dubai and another one in Qatar. He still keeps in touch with an ex-girlfriend he dated in Cairo and another in London, which you gather means he sleeps with each of them when he visits. He shows you photos of the brother with the wife on his cellphone, flips through a folder of photos and shows you the current girlfriend in Dubai (a thin, leggy blonde supermodel) and the ex in London (a thin, leggy blonde supermodel). You mention that they both look alike, and he laughs and agrees.

"I suppose I have a type," he says, not bragging at all.

More photos are displayed, one of which was taken on the beach at Fiji. The image burns into your retinas. James Bond is standing next to one of the blonde supermodel girlfriends, wearing a swimsuit, low-cut below his hips. His chest is covered with ocean sand brown hair, a treasure trail of hair leads to his trunks. There is no body fat, only lean, defined muscle. You can see every detail of his fur-covered abs. You worry you are studying the image too hard, the way you look at porn. His cellphone is burning up in your grasp, so you hand it back to him. You ask how the surfing was in Fiji on his last visit. His answer washes over you because you wonder if he thinks that you are an elderly gay man seeking affection from a younger stranger. You wonder if you will be tomorrow's joke with his brother, the wife, any of the girlfriends, current or ex.

He mentions he was hoping to take in the surf in California. He is supposed to be at a conference in San Francisco tomorrow, was planning on catching the waves at Big Sur later in the week. As he describes the differences between surfing in California and Australia, the challenges of each locale, you think about how unfair life is. Some men are born with natural, attractive gifts: handsomeness, athletic physiques, ocean sand brown hair that can be combed into rivulets. You have never felt attractively gifted. Your hair grows like cat whiskers, long, thin, invisible, and touchy. You have never been athletic. Never tried to surf, never tried to ski on water or snow. You are not a handsome spy-killing movie star. You are the sidekick, the wizard behind the screen.

After dinner Secret Agent 007 orders a nightcap for each of you. He looks at his watch, a large gold jewel that is revealed when he pulls up his sleeve. He says it is already tomorrow in Dubai.

You ask him if he is jetlagged. He answers that he only needs about four hours of sleep, so switching time zones seldom bothers him. It is another gift that separates you.

When the bill arrives, he tells the waiter to charge it to his room. He refuses the money you offer, saying it will be expensed. The company will pay for it. "You saved my life, right?" he says. "Not once but twice. What would I have done without you? You're keeping me out of trouble. My girlfriend gets so crazy when I travel."

He doesn't identify which girlfriend, and you fail to ask, because he has motioned the waiter to return to the table and take a photo of the two of you with his cellphone. "I can send her proof it was just the two of us."

You watch him type something into his cellphone. He shows you the result, a caption that reads: "SNOWPOCALYPSE WITH MY MATE!" though you are focused on how foolish you look sitting next to him. Dumpy. Dowdy. An overweight great aunt next to her Olympic-winning nephew.

But you don't show your displeasure. For years you have trained yourself to keep quiet around handsome men until something important must be noted, the true worth of any sidekick. You smile, rise from the table, hand him back his phone, and thank him for the drinks and the meal, gathering up your black winter garments to determine which layer to put on first.

"You're not abandoning me, are you, mate?" he asks. "We've got to ride this bugger out together."

Together? Did he just say *together*? Your head is light. You are unsteady on your feet. You sure you have misheard him, but he presses on. "We'll make it a Snomathon. An all-nighter. I've got some bootlegged movies we can watch. Come on. We'll make it a team effort."

An *all-nighter*? A *team effort*? His delivery is so sincere you cannot determine if he is serious or joking. Before you have put on your black sweater, he has gathered up your coat and scarf and is leading you to the elevator. There is a light ping, noting the elevator's arrival, and you follow him inside the cab. Beside him, you are frozen with fear. This wasn't the plan. The invitation was for drinks. Dinner. After dinner drinks. The only time you are ever up late is when you have insomnia.

The elevator stops at the top floor marked with a button labeled PH in the elevator. You step into a small, dimly-lit corridor where there is one door. He withdraws a card key from his pants pocket, swipes the lock, and opens the door. You step inside his suite, leaving Kansas behind. You have entered Oz.

His room is grand. Technicolor grand. A VIP suite with a formal dining area and a baby grand piano. Chinese urns.

A crystal chess set on a silver tray. Fresh flowers are in vases. There are large wicker baskets full of fruits and unhealthy snacks. While you drift toward the floor-to-ceiling windows, he is reaching for a hotel phone. When the front desk answers, he asks for room service, ordering popcorn, taco chips and guacamole, cheese and crackers, ice cream in several flavors, bottles of wine, champagne, and whiskey. You wonder who else he is inviting to join the team.

"Just like roughing it," he says, without a trace of irony. "Snowmaggedon, right?"

He disappears into a wing of the suite. You stand by the window, not knowing what to do, looking out at the snow until you see your reflection in the window. You think your head looks misshapen. Like it belongs to an alien. Thin and bald on the top. Hairy and puffy at the ears. You think of excuses to leave, ordering them in your mind:

1. You have a cat you have to feed.

2. You have a dog you have to walk.

3. You have a cactus to water.

4. You need to lose thirty pounds and restore your self-confidence before you can agree to an all-nighter with an overly attractive man with a British accent.

He returns as the informal, casually dressed spy-killing movie star. He has shed his jacket and shirt. He is wearing a white tank top that hugs his body the way you want to, displays an upper chest covered with ocean sand brown hair you want to touch. He has crime fighting arms that are tense with muscles.

"Look what I found," he says, carrying something in one hand. You deflect your attention away from the beautiful skin that surrounds his biceps to a small red-and-blue package he is holding in his palm. He is showing you a deck of playing cards. "You play poker?" he asks.

You are terrified of poker. You have no luck with cards. You cannot bluff. Your face registers every emotion even when you think you are disguising it. And you don't have twenty million dollars to lose to James Bond. You don't have a jeweled watch or an ultra-sleek red sports car that you can put up as collateral. You don't even have a dog, a cat, or a cactus that needs watering. All you have are the black urban clothes on your back. You can't imagine James Bond wanting to defeat you at strip poker.

In a tone that only canines and spy-killing movie stars can hear you suggest Gin Rummy.

"Gin Rummy," he echoes. "How fun. Let's play a few hands."

You are grateful when the idea is interrupted by a knock at the door. It is room service, a young man wheeling in the food and booze that James Bond has ordered for his team. You want to ask the young man to stay, help you defend your honor, but you see his astonished look as he drinks in the sight of James Bond in his T-shirt and crime-fighting muscles. You know he is as weak as you are. He would be useless in overcoming this spy-killing secret agent. James Bond signs the receipt, slips the young man a bill as he shakes his hand, and once again you are alone. A team of one.

James Bond eats a taco chip, says, "I love American food. Sinful. Terribly bad for you, but I suppose that's what makes it so delicious."

He sits at the table, shuffles the deck, throws them between his two hands, spins them back to the original hand, does a one-handed trick to cut the cards. He gives you a clever smile, says, "Learned that one summer in Monaco."

You win three games of Gin Rummy, he wins three, you win the seventh. He is delighted. The tacos have disappeared. He finds a jar of cashew nuts in one of the gift baskets, opens them up, pops a few into his mouth.

"You play chess, mate?" he asks.

Before you answer, he is carrying a silver tray to the table. It is an ornamental chess set. The pieces are crystal. What you noticed as an expensive decorative touch of luxury interior design, he sees as a playground.

You are the dark opponent, the royalty of black crystals. A force of evil. Urban invisible against godlike beauty. He gives you the first move. You move a pawn, so does he, and the game is underway. You capture his knight. His bishop. Another knight. He is surprised when you beat him in under ten minutes.

"An excellent opponent," he says and sets up the pieces for a rematch. You defeat him again in under ten minutes.

You are proud of your skill. Your gift. Your strategy. A combination of education, perseverance, and intelligence. One year, you came home every evening and played against your computer until you figured out a way to beat it. You ask Secret Agent 007 if he wants another rematch. You defeat him again in under ten minutes.

The cashews are gone. The ice cream is finished. He pours himself a whiskey, asks if you want another glass of wine. He is looking for your weak spot. Replaying in his mind all of his lost games.

On the fourth game you make a deliberate mistake to allow him to win. After thirty minutes of strategy, he grins. Handsomeness has triumphed. All is right with the world. "You're a gracious sport," he says, but doesn't ask for a rematch, knowing, you think, as any international crime expert knows, that you have allowed him to win. Instead, he says, "We've completely forgotten the movies."

In minutes, he has set up his laptop on the glass-topped coffee table in front of a sofa the length of the Brooklyn bridge. He arranges a bowl of popcorn at the center of the couch. He sits on one side of the bowl. You sit on the other.

The bootlegged movie is a Japanese kung fu feature. It is about a drug lord and an avenging brother, or at least that is what you think it is about. There are no subtitles. Only quick cuts and loud rock music for a soundtrack. You last for two handfuls of popcorn and then you close your eyes, wanting to find some rest.

Hours later your snoring wakes you. The popcorn bowl is empty and on the floor. Another movie is playing on the laptop, but the sound has been muted. James Bond is asleep, his head resting on your shoulder. You gather in the moment: the pressure of his body, the smell of his skin, breath, hair. You slowly shift your position, using both hands to reposition him so that he reclines fully across the sofa. You are fearful when he doesn't stir as you move him. How could he protect the world from disaster if doesn't stir at the slightest movement around him? Or perhaps he knows you are not his opponent. You are his advocate. His gadget. His sidekick. Every handsome man deserves one. Every handsome man knows when he has found one.

You close the laptop, making sure it powers off. You place the empty popcorn bowl on the room service cart. On the bottom shelf of a cabinet you find a blanket. You drape it over his sleeping body. You want to watch him, look over him, burn another image into your memory, but you are tired, thick-headed from all the food and booze.

Outside the window, in the dark Manhattan evening, the snow continues, but now, instead of falling in heavy streaks, the flakes seem to be rising up, magically back into the clouds. You think about gathering up your winter clothing, leaving your handsome host to return to your ice-cold apartment in the tenement where you live, but you know it would disappoint him, abandoning him before the adventure has been completed.

Instead you dim the lights. You walk beyond the formal dining table, the fresh flowers, the baby grand, the Chinese urns, the crystal chess set and into a bedroom. In it is the largest bed you have ever seen. The white linen is starched stiff, stretched taut across the mattress. 1200 thread count Egyptian cotton.

You are too tired to undress, to empty your pants pockets, but you lift your feet out of the snow boots you have never removed since you left your office. Cool air soaks into your damp socks. Your whole body sighs with relief. You plunge your feet beneath the bedspread.

* * *

The sun wakes you hours later. The snowing has stopped. You remain in the warmth of the bed, unable to move. The room is quiet. No sounds rise from the street. You listen to see if you can detect any movement in the other rooms of the suite, but there is nothing, not even the sound of a ticking clock.

But you think you smell coffee. You sit up in bed, pat your hair into place, slide your feet into your snow boots, feeling the pain and cramps return as you stand.

In the grand room, the couch is empty. The blanket has been folded and placed on a chair. The room service cart has been replaced with another cart. On the new one there is an urn of coffee and a set of coffee cups. On the formal dining table is a note with your name on top. You lift it up and read:

"What luck! Airport re-opened, flight not cancelled. I can make the conference in San Fran after all. If lucky I might be able to catch some waves at Big Sur!"

At the bottom is a large swirly signature. Harold Somethingoranother.

An hour later you have showered, redressed, and made the nineteen steps across a small bank of snow and are working at your desk. Snowpocalypse was a dud. Only five inches accumulated. The Hudson River is steel gray. The cliffs of New Jersey are visible. You think about sending James Bond a follow-up email, but everything you type you consider inappropriate. You are grateful when a problem surfaces in Caracas that urgently needs your attention.

* * *

Months pass. It is summer. A heat wave blankets the city. Commuters hurry home early, fearful of rolling blackouts. You are reviewing the terms of an emergency contract for Berlin when an email from Harold Somethingoranother arrives. He writes that he is stranded in the airport in Singapore. A typhoon is disrupting travel. He found the photo of the two of you together during Snowpocalypse in his cellphone and realized he had never sent you a copy.

At the bottom of his message is a link. It is an invitation from "SurfGod" to play a game of chess online.

You click the link, register for an account, creating a player named "IQ." You make the first move against your opponent. Moments later SurfGod responds, moving a pawn two spaces in front of his knight.

You play a game and win and play another and win. Your opponent sends you emails with winky faces, emoticons, and exclamation points. You only allow him to win one out of every four games played. This is your gift. Your gift to mankind.

The Devil's Cake

When my great aunt Flora Russell died at the age of ninety-eight, I was thirty-nine and still struggling to make my way in Manhattan. I had been through many rough years in the city already—trying first to be an actor, next attempting to become a playwright, but finally, finding myself in love with a wonderful guy who left me behind after a six-year relationship when he died of AIDS. I had become the beneficiary of many unpaid bills and I was unable to afford the airfare to Cincinnati and the old Victorian house on Grant Street to attend Aunt Flora's wake and funeral. A few weeks later, I was surprised when my mother's phone call caught me at my apartment on a Saturday afternoon between the three jobs I had cobbled together in order to pay my rent and living expenses.

"We're all so sorry you weren't able to fly in this weekend and help clean out your Aunt Flora's house," she said. This was my mother's backhanded way of informing me of an invitation she had neglected to pass along and expected me to refuse anyway. "Your sisters are squabbling over every piece of furniture with your cousin Shelly."

It was then that she told me about my relatives being assembled at my great aunt's house. She was calling me from the phone in the kitchen before the telephone service was cut off the following day. I asked a few tense questions about who exactly was doing the cleaning and found out that my father, uncle, brothers-in-law, and cousin's husband had rented trucks and U-hauls and were carting away items before the house

145

was put up for sale. I had flashes of memory of my great aunt's house: the steep flight of stairs to the second and third floors, the large airy kitchen with its black metal appliances and butcher block table, the fancy wing-backed parlor chairs and polished-wood end tables covered with lace doilies, and that musty, perfume-enhanced elderly woman smell everywhere throughout the house. I knew that each item in that house was vintage and antique. I couldn't entirely vouch for my cousin Shelly's adult character, but I knew my sisters had inherited many of my mother's unadmirable characteristics. My sisters Maggie and Ginger were flashing their greed to out maneuver the other and walk away with the most high-ticket items.

My silence and refusal to be drawn into this hateful game only reinforced my mother's desire for me to comment on it. She was trying to get me to say something spiteful about my sisters so she could instead put me down. My mother and I had long ago ceased pleasantries—she did not approve of my life and I did not approve of her disapproval—and it had left relations between us, well, very strained.

"Is there anything you want from the house, Jimmy?" she asked me. "To remember your Aunt Flora. Or Granny Daisy?"

"Nothing," I answered.

"Are you sure, darling? Your Daddy and I can keep it at the house till you can come down and pick it up."

"Nothing, Mother," I answered, sweeping my eyes about my small, book-cluttered city apartment. The only thing I had ever invested my meager salary in other than rent, food, basic clothing, doctor visits and medicines for Keith were the books which I had read and loved and refused to let go of. Unfortunately, I had loved many books and my tiny, overpriced studio in Greenwich Village where I had landed after Keith's death was full of them—books that both Keith and I had collected and adored. I often joked with my friends that I could open my own bookstore with all the rare items we had assembled. This was a few years before the internet had arrived and I could easily do so.

"Your sister Maggie is insistent that all the good pieces of china and silverware remain together," my mother said.

"That makes sense," I answered.

"I could send you the sugar bowl," she said, knowing, of course, that this would split the set and open up my sister's wrath. "Or the creamer."

"What would I do with those?" I laughed in response, which I knew irritated my mother more because I would not recognize the value of the china or my sister's displeasure.

"I'm just upset you are getting left out of this," my mother said with a sigh, but I knew her sentiment was not genuine. "Isn't there something in this ratty old house you want me to send you?"

"If you find a photo of Granny Daisy or Aunt Flora, that would be nice," I said, knowing that if I offered a solution, I might avoid future antagonizing.

"A photo?" my mother answered, as if I had asked, instead, for her to send me one of Aunt Flora's old hand-knit cardigan sweaters that were buried beneath mothballs in a trunk in the attic. "I don't know if I've seen any photo about of her. But if I come across one, I'll put it aside for you." She then asked if I wanted to speak to either of my sisters, and when I refused, in part because they shared my mother's sentiment over my "wasted life in New York City," the call abruptly ended.

A few weeks later a small parcel arrived at my apartment with a return address of my parents' house in Memphis. When I opened it up, I recognized it immediately. It was the old tin box Miss Gipsie had used to store her recipes and which had been on the kitchen counter at my great aunt's house. Miss Gipsie had been my great aunt's roommate, a tiny, beautiful dark-haired lady living in the third floor bedroom which had once belonged to my great great grandfather. Miss Gipsie had died during my early years in Manhattan but my mother and

Miss Gipsie had a long history of disrespect for each other. My great aunt Flora must have kept the tin box forever on the kitchen counter, and my guess was that my mother, after hanging up the phone in the kitchen after our conversation, had spied the hateful thing and decided to pass it along to me.

I lifted open the lid and looked inside. There were yellowed index cards with recipes, faded newspaper clippings, and decade-old coupons. I flipped through the items and discovered near the back a small, curled-at-the-edges black-and-white photograph of my great aunt and Miss Gipsie together in the kitchen. In an instant, I realized two things. The first was of my great aunt's deep and abiding love for Miss Gipsie. It seemed clear to me in the photograph, them candidly arm-in-arm, that they were lovers, or if not sexual lovers, then partners, a "Boston marriage" is how queer studies academics and sociologists have since described these sorts of women's relationships. And there it was, my great aunt with her short mannish haircut and gentlemanly clothes and with her arm draped around Miss Gipsie in her more feminine frills and ruffles and aprons. The other thing I immediately realized was that I had taken the photograph when I was nine or ten years-old on one of our family visits at the house. That year I had been given an "instant" camera which could produce a finished, ready-to-view photograph at the click of the button. The photographic film was pulled out of the side of the camera and if you waited long enough and stripped off a thin black paper cover, the image of the photograph would "develop" within seconds before your eyes. I had taken photos of everything on our holiday trip that year—Granny Daisy with my Dad out by the mailbox, Dad and his brother Henry in the driveway beside the car, Mother and my sisters by the Christmas tree in the parlor. I had found Aunt Flora and Miss Gipsie cooking the holiday feast in the kitchen and the two of them had stopped and posed for me. Miss Gipsie even held a wooden spoon gingerly at her side. And my thumb print was at the side of the photograph where I had hurriedly hoped to help "develop" it a little quicker.

I found a small plastic frame that was adhered to a magnet, flattened the photo, slipped it into the frame, and placed it on my refrigerator door. It gave me a small delight because I had fond memories of both Aunt Flora and Miss Gipsie and I felt that I had uncovered a skeleton in the family closet. Why had no one else remarked on their relationship in all of the years of our family going there for holiday visits? And why had this same family cast me as the evil black sheep for sharing a similar same-sex arrangement?

I looked through the other items in the tin box—recipes for green bean casserole, coq au vin, walnut stuffing, crab cakes. I unfolded and read each of them as if they were pages of a novel and it was a delightful experience. Near the back of the tin— where I had first discovered the photograph—was another aged and folded piece of paper. The creases were deep and the white paper was now golden. As I unfolded it and read it, I discovered this recipe was for "The Devil's Cake." As I looked through the ingredients I grew dizzy with astonishment. This was the recipe that had once fractured my family and I remembered the events with a rush of memory. My family *had* weighed in on Aunt Flora and Miss Gipsie's relationship. It hadn't been dismissed. I closed the box and went and studied the photograph again. My mother could not possibly have known the contents of this tin box when she sent it to me. She had sent it to me because she had hated Miss Gipsie in the very same way she had once hated my lover Keith.

* * *

My great aunt's house stripping had been organized by my father and his younger brother Henry. Granny Daisy had been my great aunt Flora's youngest sister. They were two of the six siblings born in a one-room log cabin in West Virginia at the end of the nineteenth century, whose brothers and sisters had left the hard, mountainous homestead the moment they were old enough, except for Aunt Flora who kept the household together after their mother's death and until Granny Daisy came of age. Granny Daisy was the youngest child and had been born hearing-impaired, and when she left home to attend a school for the deaf in the western part of the state, Aunt Flora and their father moved first to Cincinnati to find work in the factories and then to the old Victorian house on Grant Street, to be near Granny Daisy after she had married my grandfather, who had been deaf since contracting scarlet fever as a child, and they had joined the rest of the family in Cincinnati. When Granny Daisy had her two children—my dad and his younger brother—the family briefly moved into the Grant Street house and it was my Aunt Flora who helped take care of my dad and uncle as babies—waking up in the night to feed and change their diapers, until they were old enough to be returned and watched after by my Granny Daisy and Grampa a few blocks away. I don't know the exact sequence of events, but after my father and his brother went first to war, then to college, my Grampa died and Granny Daisy sold their house and went to live in the large house on Grant Street with Aunt Flora. I don't know exactly when my great great grandfather died or when Miss Gipsie arrived either—but she lived in the room which had once belonged to him. Aunt Flora and Miss Gipsie were always part of our family visits to see my Granny Daisy because they all shared the same house.

My mother's family was an entirely different matter. She was the middle of three daughters born to a prosperous businessman and his small town but high society wife, and this always left me with the belief that my mother had spent most of her life vying for the attention of others because she was never considered the oldest, youngest, smartest or prettiest of the sisters. Her father—my "Big Daddy" as we called him—ran a sugar company, R.B. Charles and Company—on the coast of North Carolina—and he was forever taking Big Mama and his girls on expensive cruises to South America and Cuba to visit with clients. This gave my mother worldly experiences, a hint of snobbishness, and a heightened sense of entitlement. But my mother was also deeply religious, something I think she picked up on one of her international trips, and I often believed she had developed this sort of infatuation with the Holy Spirit as a way to set herself apart from her sisters, who were more egregious and boisterous. With her own family, my mother often used religion as a weapon for instruction for her children. "Good Christians do not eat with their fingers, Jimmy," she would say to me when we were at a restaurant and I wanted to order fried chicken, or to my sisters, "Good Christians do not slouch and pout," when they were refused an ice cream dessert. As far as I was concerned Jesus didn't care whether or not I had fried chicken or that my sisters enjoyed a banana split, but after too many tantrums and screaming battles with my mother, I learned it was often easiest to suffer in Godly silence.

Holidays with Big Daddy and Big Mama were elegant and dressy affairs. There was a staff cooking and another staff serving. The china was very expensive. The silverware and glasses sparkled. There were giant crystal chandeliers hanging in the dining room and big Christmas trees and wreaths stationed throughout the finely furnished rooms of the enormous white mansion where my mother had been raised. There was always other business acquaintances invited to share cocktails and meals and the children were often dressed in their Sunday finest and asked to perform songs or play piano pieces. When Big Daddy died when I was eight, the giant house was sold to pay off a large personal and company debt, and my Big Mama relocated to a tiny apartment on the gulf coast of Florida, where she continued to complain about the "unfortunate reversal of her circumstances" until her death.

My mother's "inheritance" also disappeared, but my father had a steady job as a bank manager in suburban Memphis and his income landed us squarely in the middle class. My mother continued to pamper and impose upon her children in whatever manner she could get away with—dance lessons, horse riding lessons, band uniforms, cheerleading squads, until we were old enough to argue our own opinion on the matter and sometimes win—or at least reach an agonizing stalemate.

It was not long after Big Daddy's death that my father must have learned about his mother's fight with cancer, and so our holiday events shifted from the coast of North Carolina to the other side of the Appalachians as we made trips to Cincinnati and Grant Street to spend more time with Granny Daisy in what were expected—and were—her final years, and which was when the year of the Devil's Cake episode occurred. It wasn't the first time that Miss Gipsie and Aunt Flora made the Devil's Cake. We had tasted it before on other trips much to the extreme displeasure of our mother who labeled it "sinful" and "un-Christian"—but because we had arrived earlier than usual to spend more time with Granny Daisy—it was the first time we had witnessed them cooking it.

The recipe called for alcohol, liquor, and liqueurs—varying dried fruits and nuts soaking in small dishes of rum, wine, gin, brandy, and cognac for hours before being blended into a batter rich with eggs, butter, molasses, and more liqueur. Most of the strength and potency of alcohol would be diminished during the baking process in the oven. My dad and uncle had grown up with the holiday cake and said "it was impossible to make without getting drunk and impossible not to taste the happiness inside it." Granny Daisy, Aunt Flora, and Miss Gipsie all served the cake warm and in bowls covered with a rich cream and liqueur sauce. For years my mother had forbidden the children even a taste, but occasionally we could find one of the older women in the kitchen who would let us taste a sliver. I remember my first taste of it as one of my first memories—

and a sensation I imagine as wondrous and akin to flying in outer space.

The year we watched them make and bake it my sisters and I were all seated around the kitchen table with my cousin Shelly. Maggie, Ginger, and Shelly were coloring or helping me put together a giant picture puzzle Miss Gipsie had bought for us. Our presence in the kitchen limited the women's use of the table space to lay out their ingredients and soaking bowls, but the room was plentiful with counters and surfaces, so they set about opening cabinets, finding bottles, tasting in small spoonfuls the liqueurs that had been tucked away for a year, laughing and deciding what fruit to soak in what sauce. I don't recall them referencing a recipe—it was an entirely spontaneous event that seemed to grow more boisterous as the two women became more drunk with their tasting and oohing and aahing. There was a radio on in the kitchen and we were all singing along to Christmas carols. At some point my cousin, sisters, and I were all given "special, secret tastes" not only of the batter and the fruit but of spoonfuls of the molasses and alcohol. My mother and Aunt Gloria, Uncle Henry's wife, were talking in the "china room," a large, adjacent dining room where there was a tall hutch that housed and displayed Granny Daisy's china set which she had gotten when she married. My father and uncle were in the small front parlor talking by "signing" with Granny Daisy. All of us knew sign language because of Granny Daisy, but because the children were slower to make spelled out words into understandable sentences and phrases, there was plenty of pads and pencils scattered around the house for us all to use and help us communicate quicker if needed.

In the kitchen "Santa Claus is Coming to Town," came on the radio and Aunt Flora began singing it first to Miss Gipsie and then to us children at the table. When she reached the hook line, "Santa Claus is Coming to Town," Aunt Flora signed the phrase to us and we signed it back to her so that we were all singing both silently with our hands and loudly with our voices. Miss Gipsie joined us for the next verse and we were all signing and singing around the table. At the end of the song we loudly applauded our performance with claps and laughter. As the next song came on the radio, "Jingle Bells," the women went back to their batter and bowls and began offering us small tastes to see if the fruit was ready for the batter. This was when my mother and my Aunt Gloria entered the kitchen and my mother screamed at Aunt Flora, "In God's name, what are you doing?" And because she did not want to unleash her fury over one of her children being given a rum-soaked cranberry onto one of my father's favorite relatives, she turned and directed it at Miss Gipsie. Harsh words were tossed back and forth between the women about the abuse of children and intoxication of minors and un-Christianly behavior and bad manners and un-Godly relations between adult women. The radio was turned off. My father and uncle and Granny Daisy arrived in the kitchen. Miss Gipsie was in tears. Aunt Flora was flushed red at the face and neck. There was a flurry of angry recaps in sign language for Granny Daisy and all of us children were whisked into another room. My father and uncle had a history of sampling the cooking process of "The Devil's Cake" as young boys and found nothing out of the ordinary but my mother was relentless in her fury and indignation. There was no Devil's Cake served at Christmas dinner that year and though Miss Gipsie continued to be part of our family, continued to live and love and clean and cook with Aunt Flora every day, continued to send us children special notes and birthday cards in the mail, she never spoke another word directly to my mother for the rest of her life.

* * *

I did not acknowledge the receipt of the tin box to my mother and I did not tell her that inside it I had found the recipe for the Devil's Cake. The box found a place on my bookshelves beside an assortment of candles and souvenirs and mementos of my life in the city. Because of the strained relationship with my mother—and because of my sisters' growing families—and because of my often lack of expendable income—I only traveled to my parents' house once a year—the weekend before Thanksgiving—which left the holidays free for me to spend with my close friends and "my family of choice."

Three years after receiving Miss Gipsie's tin box, I began dating a guy named Theo. He was of Greek heritage and handsomely pudgy. We were both in our forties and somewhat set in our individual ways, but we were both looking for some kind of connection with another man and some sense of companionship: a partner to eat out with, see movies and Broadway shows together, and to catch up with at a day's end. As the holidays grew nearer and our relationship grew firmer, we discussed where we wanted to spend Thanksgiving and Christmas. I outlined my obligatory trip to my parents and Theo mentioned spending the day with his sister's family and that it would be awkward to have me there as an overnight guest. Since we had only been dating a couple of months I wasn't offended at being left out. When Christmas rolled around we faced a similar discussion, where to spend the holidays and would we spend it together. He said he usually spent the day with an old college friend named Angela who had a loft with her partner near Madison Square Park—and that every year the guests were a mix of familiar and new faces—and he thought it would be a good way to introduce me to some of his friends. I thought it was a good idea as well because my friend Marci, who I usually hooked up with on the holidays, would be out of town visiting her ill mother. Theo said that Angela's menu was entirely pot luck, but Angela and her partner Liz, who made the turkey, often suggested what other course the guests should bring—drinks, appetizers, vegetables, or dessert. As the event drew closer I asked Theo what Angela expected us to bring, and Theo announced it should be a dessert.

We had a brief discussion about where the best pies and bakeries were in the city—we both had favorites—and we both oohed and aahed over the possibilities we could find—and this was when I blithely suggested we might make the Devil's Cake and I explained the recipe to him. Theo was all giddy for the adventure of it and made me too, but since neither of us cooked on a daily basis and one of us (being me) didn't use our stove at all, he suggested we have a back-up store-bought pie in case we totally screwed it up. I photocopied the recipe and we began collecting the ingredients at his apartment. Theo lived in a large one-bedroom on the Upper West Side, his stove worked, and a realtor would describe his kitchen as an "eat in" one, so we would have enough room for the soaking bowls (and accompanying dance movements while singing along to Christmas carols and show tunes).

It was a lovely day when we made the Devil's Cake. It was cold, crisp weather so the kitchen did not overheat. We soaked the fruits, tasted the syrup and liqueurs and batter, sang along to all sorts of songs, danced and laughed and put it in the oven and passed out hours later in exhaustion. Sometime that evening I awoke on Theo's couch in a hung-over panic. Had the oven been turned off? Had we totally screwed it up?

In the kitchen I found the Devil's Cake fully baked and cooling on the counter, ready to be taken the next morning to Angela's. I assumed that Theo had risen from where he had fallen asleep on the couch and completed the project I had not been able to. I stirred him awake and we stumbled to his bedroom where we slept solidly the remainder of the night.

After showers the next morning and gathering up the ingredients we would need for the sauce, we headed down to Angela's loft. In passing, on the subway ride downtown, I had mentioned to him that I was grateful that he had woken up and turned the oven off and took the cake out. He gave me an odd look and said he thought that I had done it. A worried looked passed between us that the oven might still be on at his apartment, but I assured him it wasn't. We had spent the morning doing odd little chores in his kitchen and it would have easily been detected it if it were on.

There were fourteen for dinner and our Devil's Cake and back-up Dutch Apple pie would be enough to satisfy everyone after a large meal. After we were introduced to those Theo didn't know and I met the ones he did, we sat around a fireplace listening to music and telling small, introductory details of our lives. I had placed the Devil's Cake on a fold-out table which had been set up to hold the pot luck surprises everyone brought for the festivities. During our conversations one person or another would wander away from the fireplace and the group, fix a drink, replenish chips and crackers and cheese and dips, and then return. It was on such an occasion that Arnie, one of Angela's friends, uttered a loud, "Oh My God!" from the direction of the card table. Conversation stopped in fear as he asked with a horrified face and with large, dramatic gestures, "Who Made This Cake?"

Theo sheepishly answered that we had made it the previous day. Arnie responded with, "Oh My God! This is too divine! This is like eating solidified booze!"

We responded with relieved laughter. Arnie had taken a small bite of the Devil's Cake. I explained that the warm sauce which would be added to the small bowls later would intensify the alcoholic effect, and I recounted the joy of watching my great Aunt Flora and Miss Gipsie cooking the cake, without detailing their aborted effort.

The dessert was a terrific hit. The dinner party took a dizzying spin after it was served, everyone laughing, singing, telling one more boisterous tale after the next. If I had a penny for every photocopy I made of that recipe after that night, I would be a wealthy man. Instead, I count myself on being a happy one, because it solidified my relationship with Theo.

* * *

But my Devil's Cake tale does not end there. A few months later when I called my sister to wish her happy birthday—a call I always dreaded because it was strained with looking for safe topics to discuss such as the weather and the health of her children—I happened to mention that I had made the Devil's Cake. When Maggie asked where I had gotten the recipe with a thrill in her voice, I heard the jealousy in her response when I told her it had been tucked inside Miss Gipsie's tin box.

"You got that box?" she said, as if it had been made at Tiffany's and I hadn't deserved such a priceless inheritance. "I told Mother I wanted it."

My sister had gotten the china, the hutch, and Granny Daisy's complete bedroom suite, and because I sensed she now coveted a small, inexpensive tin box, I was of no mind to let her have it, which is what I think she expected me to do. Instead, I offered to photocopy the recipe for Devil's Cake and I did so, putting it in the mail a few days later. When the weekend before Thanksgiving rolled around and I saw her and her family at my parents' house she did not acknowledge receiving it. Of course, she did not acknowledge Theo either, and did not want to hear anything about my new partner when I tried to bring him up. My eldest sister had turned into a miniature, righteous version of our mother. I would have dismissed all of it, however, if I had not received a phone call from my younger sister Ginger about a month later, the day after Christmas, telling me that Maggie's husband, Bruce, was in the hospital and she was worried he was near death.

"She's blaming it on the Devil's Cake, you know," Ginger told me.

"What?" I asked. Theo and I had only a day before made and shared another wonderful one with friends.

"She thinks something's wrong with the recipe."

"There's nothing wrong with it," I said. "I just made it yesterday."

"She said she had cramps the moment she started making it," Ginger said, "because she thought it was... well, *excessive.*"

"But I thought Bruce..."

"He is," Ginger interrupted. "The two of them were making it together, and well, Bruce thought there was too much alcohol in the recipe, so Maggie changed it."

"Changed it?"

"She cut back on the variety of alcohol, substituted some flavored syrups instead."

"She probably put something in which had spoiled," I said. "Something that had been in her cabinets for years and she decided to get rid of by putting it into a cake. It's her own fault, if you ask me. That recipe is wonderful."

"This is just terrible, terrible," Ginger responded.

I took down the name of the hospital and the room number where my brother-in-law was resting. Ginger told me his condition was "stable" and Bruce would likely be released in a day or so. Then my younger sister added, "Mother didn't tell me you got Miss Gipsie's tin."

"I didn't know everyone had wanted it."

My younger sister had gotten Aunt Flora's bedroom suite and the dining room table and chairs.

"Dad always said that Miss Gipsie was a terrific cook," Ginger said.

"Dad says this? I've never heard him say that."

"Because you don't talk to him that much," she said, as if the root of all of our familial problems was me. The evil black sheep who liked his own sex and not the other. I always thought my mother shielded me from my father and which was the reason why my father never engaged me in conversation.

While I was on the phone with my youngest sister I went to the tin box and told her what recipes were in it and offered to photocopy them for her. Again, I had no desire to relinquish this coveted box to one of my sisters, and in a few days or so, I made good on my promise and mailed the pages to her.

That might have been the end of the story except that the years passed, my parents grew elderly, and my relations with my family grew more strained after the one attempt I made to introduce Theo into our gatherings was met with my mother's disrespect of my relationship. My mother would have no part of it and I—we—refused to show up in Memphis that year—and I think I fully learned how to put my related family aside as my family of choice grew in stature.

My father was in his late seventies and had survived a cancer scare and resulting surgery when my youngest sister Ginger decided to make the Devil's Cake. I had not been told of the occasion till after the fact. My father had told Ginger in the hospital it was the one thing he wanted to taste before he died. It was like tasting heaven, he told her. She and her eldest daughter Jenny, now in her early twenties and with two small children of her own, made the cake one afternoon and to be served the following night. It was not a holiday but my sister Ginger said that she remembered enough about the original event with Aunt Flora and Miss Gipsie to keep Jenny entertained about her being a young girl in a kitchen with her siblings and learning to sign with our Granny Daisy. "It was pure fun," Ginger said to me of her cake making experience with her daughter. "I could taste the joy and pride in that cake when we served it to him."

My father felt the cake was divine, "as good as Miss Gipsie made it," he told Ginger. My mother was reluctant to try it—I can only imagine her reasons—but she did so at the persistence of my father and to please him. That evening, back at their house, my mother took ill with what she told my father was "food poisoning." They rushed her to the hospital where she slipped into a coma, which was when I received the screeching phone call from my eldest sister Maggie.

"She's going to die," my sister wailed to me on the phone, "and all because of that damned recipe. Ginger is beside herself. She thinks that she has killed Mother."

Through my sister's sobs and gasps I pieced together the story of Ginger's cake making efforts and my mother falling ill. Maggie recounted her own efforts and her unease with the recipe and her husband's stay in the hospital. When my sister screamed at me again, that it was all my fault for digging up Miss Gipsie's recipe and trying to kill off the family because they didn't understand any of my "silly life choices," I calmly responded that Miss Gipsie and her recipe would not kill any of us.

"Your hate will do it for you," I said, "Some day, just like it is happening to Mother today."

"You don't believe that, do you?"

"Yes," I said. "Hate will eat you alive."

"That's an evil, despicable thing to say."

"I'm only saying it because I think it's the truth."

My mother died the next week. When my sister suggested that Theo not accompany me to the funeral, I declined to attend. When I finally reached my father on the phone and offered my condolences and explained my position, he responded with a resigned acceptance. "You'll visit me later, then?" he asked. "You and your friend?"

I was surprised by the invitation and his acknowledgement of Theo, and Theo and I made a trip to Memphis a few weeks later, which was the last time I saw my father. It was a nice and wonderful visit with my father and without any of my sisters around. We did not discuss the loss of my mother, nor the possibility that the Devil's Cake recipe was responsible for her death, but I do admit that my father's spirits were the best I had detected in many years. My Dad took to Theo immediately as if he were a long-lost war buddy and showed him photos of himself as a soldier in France and Germany, photos I had never seen before. I am grateful for Theo encouraging that visit. My father died not long after. I've tried many times to not let my mother's unpleasantries overwhelm my memories of her, but alas, I think my own character has failed me in that purpose, so perhaps I am her son after all, someone filled with an everlasting hate.

* * *

A few years after my father's death, my cousin Shelly was in New York with her significant other, a lovely woman named Elaine. They had been together for a little over a year but had been reluctant to share the news with other family members because the family had still considered her divorce too scandalous to accept, the "family" being primarily my sisters and their righteous offsprings. We were all in our early fifties by then and my introduction to Elaine was the couple's first attempt at coming out as gay partners. Shelly mentioned that I was an inspiration to her because I had given up my tiny downtown apartment and I and all my books had moved in with Theo and we were living as an "openly gay example to the rest of the family." Shelly and Elaine had dinner at our apartment the final night they were in Manhattan, after a whirlwind trip of sightseeing, museums, musicals, and shopping. They were a fine pair, complimenting and admiring each other, and Shelly and I acted as giddy as teenagers at discovering our newer selves.

While we were seated in the living room after the meal we had cooked—in our years living together, Theo and I had become quite good cooks, in thanks, I have always believed, to that first, successful attempt at the Devil's Cake—and I noticed Shelly's eyes scan the bookshelves we had built when I had moved in and I saw her attention rest at the old tin box.

"Miss Gipsie's box!" she said. "Isn't that remarkable. I'd know it anywhere. And here it is now and I know it!" From Aunt Flora's house, Shelly had gotten sofas from the front parlor, the butcher block kitchen table, and Miss Gipsie's dresser from the third-floor bedroom, which had been the only thing she kept when she had divorced her husband and they had sold their house.

She had not known that my mother had sent me the box, or that it had contained Miss Gipsie's recipes or the alleged one which had almost killed my brother-in-law or had done in my mother according to my sister Maggie.

"Remember those meals that she and Aunt Flora used to cook!" Shelly said. "Oh my, they were so delicious."

I told her I had many of Miss Gipsie's recipes and which were still in the tin box and that I would be glad to share any one of them with her. The two women smiled and said that sounded wonderful. "Shelly talked about them often when we first met," Elaine said. "They were really a couple?" she asked.

"I believe so," I said, and I went and found the framed picture magnet that was now on our refrigerator. The two women admired the other two women and I told my cousin Shelly I would have a copy of the photograph made for her.

"And that pudding they made together with the sauce?" Shelly asked, as if a flash of memory surfaced. "What was it called?"

I told her it was called "The Devil's Cake" and that I also had the recipe. Theo nodded and said we made it every year for friends and it was always a dizzying success. For the next few minutes I told Shelly and Elaine about my sisters' disastrous attempts with the recipe and its supposed relation to my mother's death. She and Elaine listened in awe.

"That's nonsense," Shelly said at the conclusion of the tales, and asked if I would give her the recipe. "I know a few relatives I wouldn't mind killing off, though, if it is true."

"We both do," Elaine added and laughed.

I told her they could have Miss Gipsie's tin box and that the recipe was inside it and that I was glad to pass it along to a family member who now needed it. I went to the bookshelf and took the tin box and slipped it into Shelly's hands.

She held it, smiling, and offered a small sigh of thanks.

The conversation continued for a minute or so, small recollections between Shelly and I about Miss Gipsie and Aunt Flora.

"What about the recipe?" Elaine asked, interrupting us with alarm. "Don't you want to keep it? Make a copy of it before you hand it over?"

"Of course not," I answered, tossing a sly glance across the room at Theo. "We both know it by heart."

"The best thing about this recipe is that it is foolproof," my partner added. "Make it with a lot of joy and be sure to get drunk doing so," he said. "And that's how wonderful it will taste."

Why Didn't Someone
Warn You
About
Prince Charming?

You were never supposed to reach sixty. You survived a premature birth, the AIDS decades, the Y2K bug, 9/11, four hurricanes, three broken ribs, and two heart attacks. You don't know whether to feel grateful or cursed. You are counting the days down to retirement, though according to your savings and investment accounts, those days are decades away. You are not greedy or needy. You only want one year of retirement and then Fate can snap the door shut. But even that diagnosis is grim. Your last heart attack left you with unresolved complications. Some days are fine. Others you are short of breath. Your heart is too large and works too slow. Every step is a concern.

But you refuse to let your lack of good health discourage you. You still believe happiness is around the corner, the check is in the mail, and the ship is about to dock. You still plan to learn a foreign language, take art classes, and walk on every continent. At sixty-three you have a list of places you have never visited. Every day you check the cost of flights to Tokyo or Dublin or Barcelona or Vienna. You search available hotel rooms on the internet: deluxe, luxury, superior, and platinum accommodations. Your email is flooded with travel deals from cruise lines, hotel chains, and tour operators because you subscribe to every offer of a coupon or discount that comes your way. Nothing, however, matches up with your budget and bank account. So you consider alternatives: a weekend in Vermont, an overnight in the Poconos, a day trip to Philadelphia. You think about asking someone to go with you to share some of the expenses and then you rethink that option. Everyone you know is too full of their own advice, critical of tiny details, and know a better way for you to live your life. After traveling for years with friends, boyfriends, lovers, siblings, and parents, you prefer to see the world solo. The journey is yours; the experience remains personal.

You have no regrets. You think you have always chosen the right path. Nostalgia only arrives at night when you are alone and on the second glass of wine. You sit in front of your laptop and Google the names of ex-boyfriends, ex-lovers, and ex-tricks, reading their posts on Facebook and Twitter and Instagram, studying their profiles and relationship status. One ex is now a senior vice president at the Disney Channel; another is a landscape architect in Pennsylvania. One ex has a partner who sings in an all-gay male choir who posts videos that make you weep; another has a partner who deconstructs the current political climate in succinct tweets which elicit both praise and hate. You study likes and emojis and friends lists, looking for anyone you might share in common. This is how you discover Prince Charming is still alive. The man who broke your heart and then cashed the check.

You were twenty-eight and out of work when you answered an ad that had been handwritten on a notecard and tagged to the bulletin board at the entrance of a gay bar in Greenwich Village: a Greek financier was looking for a courier. Payment would be made in cash. Only a passport was required. You had friends who couriered for free trips abroad and this was something just like they were doing, only better because the end result was a trip *and* cash in your pocket. You called the number on the notecard and arranged to meet the financier at an Upper East Side apartment. He was forty-one and incredibly sleek and handsome, a cousin of the deposed Greek royal family. Prince Nicholas Kocolatus. You slept with him to get the job, though you would have slept with him even if there wasn't a job. You had stars in your eyes. He was a ladder you could climb. You told all of your friends and ex-boyfriends you still spoke to that you had finally met your Prince Charming. Where was everyone's advice when you needed it? Why didn't someone warn you about Prince Charming?

You slept with the Prince for a week before he gave you your first assignment. He said he was negotiating a loan between international parties. He gave you a plane ticket to Geneva and an envelope to deliver to a bank. The bank would issue you cash upon receipt of the envelope and the cash would be for your salary, your overnight hotel room, and your return plane fare to New York.

Thirty-five years later you discover Prince Charming on Facebook. He now goes by the name Nick Koco. He is seventy-six years old and still has a full head of hair. He doesn't admit to being of royalty, his work experience is not detailed, and there is no mention of where he now lives, but he has a partner in Palm Springs. Sergio Donnola admits to being thirtysomething though by the lighting in his photos he looks to be late sixties. His profile says that he has been in a relationship with Nick for forty-one years.

Forty-one years?

You stare at Sergio's photographs. You save them to your hard drive and open them up with a software program that allows you to enlarge them. You stare some more at Sergio's photos. You realize that you have met him before. His evil grin has been burned into your memory. Take away the jowls and the capped teeth and the skin bronzer and the hair implants and thirty-five years ago Sergio was the young man you handed the envelope to in the lobby of the bank in Geneva.

Your first impression is astonishment. Your second is rage. Thirty-five years ago when you asked Sergio in the lobby of the bank in Geneva about the cash you were supposed to receive, he gave you that evil smirk and said, "There must be some mistake."

There was no mistake. It was a set up. A sting. You couriered illegal funds and then had to pay the price of your own trip. Before he disappeared you threatened to report Sergio to the police. "And tell them what?" he said and laughed at you.

Thirty-five years later the anger and humiliation return. When you finally made it back to New York Prince Charming was nowhere to be found. The doorman who let you in and out of the Upper East Side building said the tenants had been abroad for more than a couple of years. He did not know of anyone who had been living in the apartment. There was no Kocolatus in the phone book. There were no census records of his existence. You vowed revenge on everyone, even if the form of it was sending out bad karma, muttering curses, and sticking pins in homemade Voodoo dolls. Then you vowed to never speak of it again and wipe it off of your history. Prince Charming was not even an anecdote.

You pour yourself another glass of wine. You Google their names. You search other browsers and other records. Sergio is an interior designer though you cannot find details on any designs or portfolios or clients. Prince Charming runs an online art gallery whose website is inaccessible. A blank canvas. How have you never discovered any of this before? On Facebook you see that they are headed next weekend to Las Vegas to "celebrate their fifth anniversary" of being married to each other. You think there should be a law in place to stop that. Scammers should not be allowed to marry scammers.

* * *

The flight to Vegas was quicker than the process through the airport security. Your hotel has a marble lobby with fountains and your room has a terrific view of the pool. There is a noisy casino, an early bird buffet, and monorails to other hotels and casinos. When you checked in you asked if Mr. Koco had arrived. The clerk said he did not see a reservation with that name. You wonder if they booked under Sergio's last name or if they are scamming the hotel the same way they scammed you thirty-five years ago.

You unpack in your room and return to the lobby and wait, hoping to catch their arrival. With your cellphone you check their social media accounts but there are no updates. You don't have a plan. You don't know what you will say when you confront them. You don't want to start drinking yet and tire yourself out in case you decide to spring into some kind of action. So you take a seat in an oversized chair and close your eyes and practice your yoga breathing. Soon you are asleep in the lobby.

Your snoring wakes you. You have been out for almost an hour. You realize you have drooled on your shirt. You look around the lobby and assess the scenario. You are invisible to everyone because of your age, weight, and lack of hairline.

You take the elevator to the spa, thinking you might have a massage. You change at a locker and sit in the men's sauna. Everything is white marble and white tile and white clouds of steam. Slippers are recommended and are available in the locker room. Men wander in and out of the room where the hot tub is located. Behind you are showers, a door to the steam room and a door to the dry sauna. You remember your youth, the nights you roamed the baths on the Lower East Side with only a towel around your waist. Happiness was always right around the corner. You take a seat in the hot tub, even though you are aware that it may cause your heart to work too hard.

Here, you remain invisible. The security cameras in every corner of the room do not record you. Someone watching you is not really watching you. An overweight elderly balding man has no appeal to anyone.

In the hot tub you think about the cost of the plane ticket to Geneva and the hotel room thirty-five years ago. You add in compounded interest, penalties and fines, and more compounded interest. In an alternate world where you could collect what was due to you because justice was blind, you would now be a wealthy man.

You begin to feel dehydrated. Your skin is more wrinkled than usual. You hop out of the hot tub, leaving a trail of puddles on the white tiles of the floor. You rinse off in the shower and change back into your clothes at your locker. From the courtesy phone you call the front desk and ask if Mr. Donnola has checked in. The clerk says there is no one by that name with a reservation. You hang up and wonder if they decided on another hotel. Or if they canceled their trip.

You take the elevator to the buffet. You eat a lot. Then you eat more. Then you eat dessert. A waiter brings you another glass of wine. You think about how wonderful Las Vegas is. A few minutes later you are in your hotel room deep asleep.

* * *

The next morning you wake early, earlier than usual because of the time difference. On your cellphone you check the weather, your email, and Prince Charming's social media accounts.

Nothing.

You take the elevator down to the gym where you walk on a slow pace on the treadmill until your head clears. Back in your room you shower and shave and dress in shorts and a T-shirt and a straw hat because you think you might float along the monorails after breakfast.

In the hotel dining room you sit at an empty table near the window and have breakfast. You are surprised when you see the scammers sitting at a nearby table. You are suddenly short of breath. You practice your yoga breathing, slow inhales and exhales of breaths. You would recognize Prince Charming anywhere, even at this old age. But if you hadn't done your homework, you would never know who was seated opposite him.

You look harder to find their faults. Prince Charming stoops a little. His hair is dyed a solid helmet of black. You realize he is wearing a wig. His spotted hands shake as he reaches for a coffee cup. But he is dressed in an expensive elegant gray shirt and slacks.

Sergio has a scruffy beard that has been dyed an orange-brown. He has lots of bling on his wrists and fingers and around his neck. You place the two of them into context of this hotel in Las Vegas and the white marble and fountains and wonder if you misjudged them. Maybe they are not scammers. Maybe they are mafia. Don Corleone and Sancho Panza way-way-way-way off-Broadway.

You try to overhear their conversation. You make quick glances to see if you can read their lips. You use your cellphone camera to zoom in on them. They don't seem to even be talking to each other. In fact, you find them dull and boring and realize that that is how they also feel about each other. They pay no notice to you. You remain invisible to them. Only your eyes would betray you so you keep them focused on your cellphone until they need to be focused elsewhere.

You follow them out of the restaurant and into the casino. Prince Charming settles in front of a slot machine with a plastic bucket of quarters. Sergio wanders through the aisles and settles at a blackjack table. You watch him lose a round. Then you buy a roll of quarters and sit near Prince Charming.

You lose your money quickly. You save some quarters for later, hiding them deep in your pockets in the hope that you will never find them so that you will not have to lose them in a slot machine. The noise in the casino is annoying. You look at Prince Charming and wish he had taken the bus to see the Hoover Dam because you could have pushed him off the ledge.

You imagine other ways of doing him in. Maybe you could topple a slot machine on him. Maybe you could kidnap him and shove him off the north rim of the Grand Canyon.

Suddenly you are depressed. This is not who you are. This is not how you wish to be remembered. This is not your idea of a vacation in Vegas. You stand up and wonder if it is not too late to take the day trip into the desert. You rush out of the casino and are relieved to see that there is no line at the concierge's desk.

* * *

It is late when you return to the hotel. You have missed the early bird buffet. A concert has already started. The trip to the desert was long and relaxing. You have a heavy bag of souvenirs. You have forgotten all about the amateur Don Corleone and Sancho Panza.

You take your souvenirs to your room and then take the elevator to the spa. You change out of your clothes at a locker and head to the hot tub with a towel and a pair of slippers.

You sit in the tub until you are dehydrated and wrinkled. You leave a puddle of water on the floor as you step into your slippers and walk to a nearby shower stall to rinse off.

Behind you, over the sound of the running water, you hear voices. There is some kind of an argument. You feel the ground shake with a thump thump thud. A man's voice yells, "Nickie! Nickie!"

You turn off the shower. You listen for a millisecond. Or maybe a minute. Or maybe even longer. You hear heavy breaths and gasps and sobs.

You wrap a towel around your waist and step into your slippers and look around the corner of the shower stall.

You see Prince Charming sprawled on the floor beside the hot tub. His feet are bare. In fact, he is entirely nude. He must have slipped in the puddle of water you left. Sergio is also nude. He is sitting on the floor, cradling Prince Charming's head in his lap.

Sergio looks up from the floor and meets your eyes. "Help," he says. "Can you call for help?"

* * *

You complain to the hotel management. The marble tiles in the spa are too slick and slippery. A detective arrives to question you about the fatalities. Hotel security does not even have a record of you on the video of the incidents. He asks where you were at the time of the tragedy. After you tell him that the hotel should not even think about installing video cameras in shower stalls, you ask the detective why there are no rubber mats in the spa. No anti-slip tape. No hand rails. No staff on duty. Surely there must be regulations in place for a common space like this. He says he will follow up with hotel management.

A few minutes later you tell the hotel management that this is all too distressing. Your trip has been ruined. They offer you upgrades and discounts. You berate them for trying to take advantage of your depression and the fatal scenario you have witnessed and which is now burned into your memory.

You stay an extra day at the hotel, courtesy of the hotel. You dine at the early bird buffet, paid by the hotel. You take in a concert, gratis of the hotel. That evening, you return to your room and fall easily asleep.

The next morning before you check out of the hotel to take your free flight back to New York, you go to the casino. You find six quarters left in your pocket. You play the quarters in a slot machine. You win seven dollars' worth of quarters. You play them all. On the last five quarters you make wishes, but you come up empty. You have lost it all. As you step away from the slot machine you slide your hands deeper into your pants and find one quarter in the pocket you did not check.

You return to the slot machine and slide your quarter into the slot. You win Big Time. All cash. Enough to retire early.

Acknowledgments

Some of the stories in this work were originally published, in different versions, in the following: "Lancelot's Secret" first appeared in the anthology *ImageOutWrite, Vol. Five* and *Off the Rocks: An Anthology of GLBT Writing, Vol. 20*. "Mr. Darcy's Pride" first appeared in *Saints and Sinners 2018: New Fiction from the Festival*. "How to Obtain an Alfred Hitchcock Physique (and Bonus Dark Psyche)" first appeared in *The Flexible Persona*. "My Adventure with Tom Sawyer" first appeared in *Best Gay Romance 2014* and was reprinted in *Best Gay Stories 2015*. "My Night with Rudolph Valentino" first appeared in *Next*. "What Would Q Do?" first appeared in *Mad Scientist Journal*. "Sometimes You Have to Settle for Popeye (Even Though You'd Rather Play with Bluto)" and "The Devil's Cake" first appeared in *Chelsea Station*.

Jameson Currier

Jameson Currier is the author of seven novels: *Where the Rainbow Ends*; *The Wolf at the Door*; *The Third Buddha*; *What Comes Around*; *The Forever Marathon, A Gathering Storm,* and *Based on a True Story*; five collections of short fiction: *Dancing on the Moon; Desire, Lust, Passion, Sex; Still Dancing: New and Selected Stories; The Haunted Heart and Other Tales*; and *Why Didn't Someone Warn You About Prince Charming?*; and a memoir: *Until My Heart Stops*. His short fiction has appeared in many literary magazines and websites, including *Velvet Mafia, Confrontation, Christopher Street, Genre, Harrington Gay Men's Fiction Quarterly,* and the anthologies *Men on Men 5, Best American Gay Fiction 3, Certain Voices, Boyfriends from Hell, Men Seeking Men, Best Gay Romance, Best Gay Stories, Wilde Stories, Unspeakable Horror, Art from Art,* and *Making Literature Matter.* His AIDS-themed short stories have also been translated into French by Anne-Laure Hubert and published as *Les Fantômes,* and he is the author of the documentary film, *Living Proof: HIV and the Pursuit of Happiness.* His reviews, essays, interviews, and articles on AIDS and gay culture have been published in many national and local publications, including *The Washington Post, The Los Angeles Times, Newsday, Lambda Book Report, The Gay and Lesbian Review, The Washington Blade, Bay Area Reporter, Frontiers, The New York Native, The New York Blade, Out,* and *Body Positive.* In 2010 he founded Chelsea Station Editions, an independent press devoted to gay literature, and the following year launched the literary magazine *Chelsea Station*, which has published the works of more than two hundred writers. The press also serves as the home for Mr. Currier's own writings which now span a career of more than four decades. Books published by the press have been honored by the Lambda Literary Foundation, the American Library Association GLBTRT Roundtable, the Publishing Triangle, the Saints and Sinners Literary Festival, the Gaylactic Spectrum Awards Foundation, and the Rainbow Book Awards. A self-taught artist, illustrator, and graphic designer, his design work is often tagged as "Peachboy." Mr. Currier has been a member of the Board of Directors of the Arch and Bruce Brown Foundation, a recipient of a fellowship from New York Foundation for the Arts, and a judge for many literary competitions. He currently divides his time between a studio apartment in New York City and a farmless farmhouse in the Hudson Valley.